Alex knew the mon ... *eyes left him.*

It was a damned relief.

And he did a good job of not staring at her. He kept his head forward, staying focused on his sister.

At least until the minister addressed Gray. "Will you love her and comfort her, honor and keep her...?"

Alex shifted his gaze a little to the left so he could catch sight of Cassandra in his peripheral vision. She was wearing a spectacular dark red jacket and skirt combo that fit her body as if made for it.

Will you love her...?

I will, he thought. All the days of my worthless life.

And he wanted to comfort her. He just couldn't do that without dishonoring her and his dead friend. Not knowing how he felt.

Knowing what he'd done...

Dear Reader,

This beautiful month of April we have six very special reads for you, starting with *Falling for the Boss* by Elizabeth Harbison, this month's installment in our FAMILY BUSINESS continuity. Watch what happens when two star-crossed high school sweethearts get a second chance—only this time they're on opposite sides of the boardroom table! Next, bestselling author RaeAnne Thayne pays us a wonderful and emotional visit in Special Edition with her new miniseries, THE COWBOYS OF COLD CREEK. In *Light the Stars,* the first book in the series, a frazzled single father is shocked to hear that his mother (not to mention babysitter) eloped—with a supposed scam artist. So what is he to do when said scam artist's lovely daughter turns up on his doorstep? Find out (and don't miss next month's book in this series, *Dancing in the Moonlight).* In Patricia McLinn's *What Are Friends For?,* the first in her SEASONS IN A SMALL TOWN duet, a female police officer is reunited—with the guy who got away. Maybe she'll be able to detain him this time....

Jessica Bird concludes her MOOREHOUSE LEGACY series with *From the First,* in which Alex Moorehouse finally might get the woman he could never stop wanting. Only problem is, she's a recent widow—and her late husband was Alex's best friend. In Karen Sandler's *Her Baby's Hero,* a couple looks for that happy ending even though the second time they meet, she's six months' pregnant with his twins! And in *The Last Cowboy* by Crystal Green, a woman desperate for motherhood learns that "the last cowboy will make you a mother." But real cowboys don't exist anymore...or do they?

So enjoy, and don't forget to come back next month. Everything will be in bloom....

Have fun.

Gail Chasan
Senior Editor

Please address questions and book requests to:
Silhouette Reader Service
U.S.: 3010 Walden Ave., P.O. Box 1325, Buffalo, NY 14269
Canadian: P.O. Box 609, Fort Erie, Ont. L2A 5X3

FROM THE FIRST

JESSICA BIRD

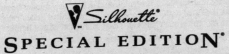

SPECIAL EDITION®

Published by Silhouette Books

America's Publisher of Contemporary Romance

To Stacy Boyd, with so many thanks

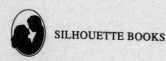 SILHOUETTE BOOKS

ISBN 0-373-24750-8

FROM THE FIRST

Copyright © 2006 by Jessica Bird

This edition published by arrangement with Harlequin Books S.A.

® and TM are trademarks of Harlequin Books S.A., used under license.
Trademarks indicated with ® are registered in the United States Patent
and Trademark Office, the Canadian Trade Marks Office and in other
countries.

Visit Silhouette Books at www.eHarlequin.com

Printed in U.S.A.

Books by Jessica Bird

Silhouette Special Edition

Beauty and the Black Sheep #1698
His Comfort and Joy #1732
From the First #1750

* *The Moorehouse Legacy*

JESSICA BIRD

graduated from college with a double major in history and art history, concentrating on the medieval period. Which meant she was great at discussing anything that happened before the sixteenth century, but not all that employable in the real world. In order to support herself, she went to law school and worked in Boston in healthcare administration for many years.

She now lives in the South with her husband and her beloved golden retriever. As a writer, her commute is a heck of a lot better than it was as a lawyer and she's thrilled that her professional wardrobe includes slippers and sweatpants. She likes to write love stories that feature strong, independent heroines and complex, alpha male heroes. Visit her Web site at www.JessicaBird.com and e-mail her at Jessica@JessicaBird.com.

Dear Reader,

I have so loved spending time with the Moorehouses and hope you have enjoyed their stories as well. Love and family are the things that make life worth living and I think that Frankie, Joy and Alex each learned how true that is.

Just to let you know, Spike and Madeline are going to run into each other again very soon! And boy...you want to talk about fireworks? The two of them are spectacular together. Oh, and by the way, Sean O'Banyon has a woman in his future, too. (And so do his two handsome brothers, Billy and Mac...)

Thanks so much for reading! And I'd love to hear from you!

Jess
Jessica@JessicaBird.com

Chapter One

Alex Moorehouse had no intention of answering the knock on the bedroom door. Flat on his back and halfway through a Harry Potter hardcover, he wasn't in the mood for company.

Not that he ever was, but at this moment he really didn't want to deal with anybody. He'd actually managed to find a position for the cast on his lower leg that relieved the pain. Or at least dulled it so he could concentrate on something else. Having a measure of peace in his body was so rare he didn't want it frayed by an intruder.

It had been almost three months since he'd felt strong, able. Himself. Three months, four surgeries, and a post-op infection that had nearly killed him. Enough hell to wipe clean most, but not all, of his transgressions.

There were at least two sins he would have to repay in the real Hades.

The knocking came again. He kept silent.

The way he figured it, the fire department wouldn't bother with formalities, so nothing was up in flames. If it was an EMT, he was pretty sure they were looking for someone else because he was breathing, so he wasn't dead. And if it was one of his sisters, they would be back.

God knew, they always came back. Those two women were in and out of the room constantly. Trying to feed him. Coaxing him to come downstairs. Riding him about going to a grief counselor.

He loved them. And he wished they'd leave him the hell alone.

The door opened a crack. Joy, the younger one, stuck her head in.

He watched her eyes go to the liquor bottle on the floor next to the bed. It was a reflex with them both. Open the door. Check the scotch level. Door open. Scotch check.

He thought about dropping a pillow to hide the single malt, but figured that little defensive maneuver would only draw more attention to the damn thing.

So he just stared at her, waiting.

This was going to be good. Joy looked like she was about to jump out of her skin.

"You, ah, you have someone who wants to see you."

He had to clear his throat before he could speak.

"No, I don't." God, he sounded hoarse. That scotch was doing a number on his vocal cords, and he wondered how his liver was faring.

"Yes, you—"

"And I know this because I haven't invited anyone here."

The way he saw it, one of the advantages to staying in someone else's house was that nobody could find you.

Friends, colleagues. Reporters. Hell, if you kept your yap shut, you could practically fall off the side of the earth.

Which was a trip he was dying to make.

All things considered, he should be thanking the fire that had made his family's bed-and-breakfast, White Caps, uninhabitable. In the aftermath, Joy's fiancé, Gray, had taken all the Moorehouses in, and although Alex hated being a mooch, he was grateful for the anonymity he'd been granted.

Besides, this particular hideout was a classy one.

Gray Bennett's place in the Adirondacks was a fricking palace and the guest room Alex had been crashing in for the past six weeks was as tricked up as the rest of the mansion. Top-tier everything, from the antiques to the rugs, not that Alex could name the particulars. He was about as far away from the *Queer Eye for the Straight Guy* types as a man could get. Wouldn't know an Aubusson from an Audubon.

Bennett, on the other hand, had superb taste. Which explained why he wanted to marry Alex's little sister.

"Alex—"

He refocused. "There anything else?" He cocked an eyebrow.

Joy pushed a length of hair back, her ruby engagement ring flashing. "It's Cassandra."

The sound of the name brought Alex's eyelids crashing down.

In a relentless stream of flashbacks, he saw the woman he had loved from the first moment he'd met her six years ago. Her dark red hair and pale green eyes. Her flashing smile. Her incomparable elegance.

Her wedding ring.

Guilt hit him like a train, sending him deep into the nightmare.

He was back on the sailboat, back in the storm. Fighting against the wind and the horizontal rain. Holding on to his best friend's hand. Feeling that grip slip until his partner was lost to the hungry sea. He saw himself screaming into the darkness until his voice was gone. Searching the waves with a spotlight, looking for a man in the ocean.

On that horrible night, the wheel of fate had been spun and everyone had lost. Reese Cutler had died. Cassandra Cutler had become a widow. And Alex had been sealed in a coffin of self-hatred he was never going to get out of.

"Is she staying in this house through your wedding?" he asked tightly.

"Yes."

Alex pushed his palms into the mattress and hefted his upper body to the vertical. Everything hurt so he lay back down. "Then I'm leaving."

"Alex, you can't."

"Watch me." He didn't care if he had to drag himself back onto Moorehouse property. Their father's old workshop had a potbellied stove and a bathroom. Combined with a total lack of phone lines, the place was good enough for him.

"But you promised you wouldn't move into the shop until you saw the doctor—"

"I'm meeting with the orthopedist on Monday. Seventy-two hours is close enough."

Joy's eyes drifted to the floor.

"Alex, I...I was hoping we could all be under the same roof for my wedding," she said softly. "You, me and Frankie. It's been so long since you've been home. And after the fire—"

Alex cursed. "Stop. Just stop."

Damn it, he had a terrible feeling his escape route was getting cut off. As much of a selfish hard-ass as he was, he wasn't about to be one more disappointment during what should have been a happy time for Joy. After all, White Caps was uninhabitable following the fire in its kitchen. Most of her stuff had been destroyed in the blaze as the family's rooms were in the old staff quarters in the back. And he had to imagine she was missing both their dead parents more than ever.

God, had it been ten years since the two of them had died out on the lake?

"Alex, please say you'll stay."

"If I do," he said roughly, "I'm not seeing that woman."

"She just wants to talk with you."

"Then tell her I'll call her later." Like in a decade. Or five.

"You could do that yourself." There was a long pause. "She's hurting, just like you are. She needs some support."

"Not from me, she doesn't."

The last thing that widow needed was sympathy from someone who'd lusted after her for years; who'd watched her from the shadows with greed, seeing her as both a miracle and a curse; who'd lain awake wondering what her skin would feel like, what her mouth would taste like.

Hell, she deserved comfort from a man who had more honor than he did, someone who hadn't fallen in love with his best friend's wife.

And who just might have… God, he couldn't even bear the thought of what he'd done.

Alex shut his eyes. Nausea, his constant companion of late, made his empty stomach swell like a trash bag left in the heat.

"Alex—"

"I've got nothing to offer her," he spat. "So tell her to stay away from me."

Joy recoiled. "How can you be so cruel?"

"Because I'm a bastard, that's how."

When the door shut, Alex slowly sat up again. His head spun and his eyes pounded. Using his good arm, he picked up his leg by its cast and moved it off the bed. Then he carefully braced his weight on one of his crutches and cantilevered himself into a standing position. He hobbled over to a mirror.

He looked scary. Bloodshot, red-rimmed eyes with bags under them. Sallow pallor. Sunken cheeks. Whiskers.

He was fading away, he thought.

But then unrelenting guilt, and enough time in an OR so he was almost a surgical resident, would do that to a guy.

He looked down at his leg. In a couple days, he'd know whether he was keeping it or having it amputated below the knee. That shiny new titanium rod they'd used to replace his tibia hadn't taken after the first implantation, and when the orthopedic surgeon operated again six weeks ago, the woman had made it clear. They'd take one more shot at it and then it was saw time.

Okay, so she hadn't been that blunt.

Not that the outcome really mattered to him. Either way, with an artificial limb or a reconstructed lower leg, his future wasn't clear. As a professional America's Cup sailor, and captain of the best crew in the sport, he needed both his body and his mind in top shape. Neither were there. Not by a long shot. And even if they fixed his leg, it wasn't as if they were doing cranial transplants.

The knocking started up again.

"I told you I wasn't going to see her," he growled.

"So I heard." Through the door, Cassandra's voice was low.

Alex shut his eyes. Dear Lord.

Cassandra Cutler put her forehead on the doorjamb.

He sounded exactly the same. Impatient. Commanding. And not at all interested in having anything to do with her.

Alex Moorehouse had never liked her—something that had been horribly awkward considering he'd been her husband's sailing partner. Best friend. Confidant.

Reese had tried to reassure her that Alex was just a gruff kind of guy, but she knew it was personal. The man had always gone out of his way to avoid her, and whenever that was impossible, he glowered. At first she'd thought he was being territorial over Reese, but as time passed she'd realized that was too petty for someone like Alex. He simply couldn't stand the sight of her, though what she'd done to offend him she couldn't guess.

So she shouldn't be surprised he wouldn't see her now. And she really wasn't.

It just hurt. Although exactly why, she wasn't sure. On so many levels, it didn't matter that Alex Moorehouse thought she was beneath him. She was never going to run into him again, not anymore. He was nothing in the larger scheme of her life.

Except she'd always hoped the man would come around and see her as more than just an irritating hanger-on. Alex had this way about him that suggested if he liked you, you'd passed some kind of stringent test.

With his discipline and his rigor, his rugged body and his fierce intellect, he was all about high standards, for himself and others. It was obvious why his crew both worshipped and feared him, why even Reese had had stars in his eyes when he'd talked about the great Alex Moorehouse.

Suddenly the door jerked open.

She looked up. And had to cover her mouth with her hand at what she saw. "Oh…my God."

Alex had always been larger than life. A big, muscular man, with eyes like a dangerous animal and an aura like the sun. She'd been totally intimidated when she'd first met him, this sailing phenomenon her husband had revered, this hard man the international America's Cup community called The Warrior.

The person standing in front of her in a T-shirt and pajama bottoms was half-dead. Alex's skin hung off his bones, as if he'd eaten little in the three months since the accident, and he was leaning on a crutch, one leg in a cast. His sunken cheeks were brushed with beard. His thick, sun-streaked hair, always clipped tight like a military man's, was now shaggy.

But his eyes. His dark blue eyes were what affected her most. They were dull in his harsh face. Flat as stone. Even the color seemed to have dimmed.

"Alex…" she whispered. "My God… Alex."

"Yeah, I'm gorgeous, aren't I?"

He hobbled back to the bed, as if he couldn't hold himself up any longer, and he moved as an old person would, with deliberate thought and anticipation. It seemed as though his body was a house of cards, capable of falling to pieces if he wasn't careful.

"May I help you?" she asked.

His response was a glare over his shoulder as he put the crutch aside and slowly sank onto the mattress. She watched as he maneuvered his leg up using his arms. When he settled back against the pillow, he was breathing heavily and he closed his eyes.

She had a feeling he'd be cursing from the pain if she hadn't been in the room.

Good heavens, this was not at all what she'd imagined seeing him would be like.

"I've been…worried about you," she said.

His eyelids flipped open. But he stared at the ceiling, not at her.

The silence that followed was thick and cold as snow.

She came into the room a little. Shut the door quietly. "I have a reason for needing to see you."

Nothing. No response.

"Ah, did Reese ever tell you about his will?"

"No."

"He left you—"

"I don't want money."

"The boats."

Alex's face turned toward her briefly. His lips were tight. "What?"

"All twelve of them. The two America's Cups, the schooner, his antique four-master. The others… All of them."

Alex put one hand over his eyes. The muscle in his jaw worked as if he were grinding his molars.

She noted absently that he was still built strong, even with the weight loss. On the arm he had up, his biceps were curled thickly, stretching the short sleeve of his T-shirt, and his solid forearms had a network of veins running down them.

Her eyes drifted to his chest and then on to his taut stomach. The T-shirt had ridden up as he'd lain down, revealing a thin stripe of hair that ran from his belly button into the waistband of the pajama bottoms.

She looked back to his face quickly.

"I thought you should know," she said. "The estate is being probated, but it's a large, complicated one so it'll take some time. My point being, you won't have to worry about storage fees for a while."

There was another long silence.

His sisters had warned her that he wasn't letting anyone inside, and they'd been very right. But when had he ever? She could remember Reese saying he knew his partner's character like the back of his hand, but the man's thoughts and feelings were totally off-limits.

"So I guess I'll… I'm going to go," she said finally.

When her hand was on the doorknob, she heard Alex clear his throat. "He loved you. You know that, don't you?"

Tears leaped into her eyes as she glanced back at him. God, he was so still. "Yes."

Alex's head turned slowly. And he looked at her.

Agony was in his face. Total, abject despair. The depth of the searing emotion floored her, and she came across the room on impulse.

Which was a bad idea.

He shrank from her. Actually pushed his body away, right to the far edge of the mattress.

Cassandra skidded to a halt next to the bed and fought not to completely break down.

"I will never understand why you've hated me all these years," she said, her voice cracking.

"That was never the problem," he shot back. "Now, please, just leave. It's better for us both."

"Why? You were his best friend. I was his wife."

"You don't need to remind me of that."

Cassandra shook her head and gave up. "The lawyers will be in touch about your inheritance."

She closed the door behind her and quickly went down the hall to the guest room she'd been given. Sitting on the edge of the bed, she straightened a fold in her Chanel skirt, put her hands in her lap, crossed her legs at the ankles—

And sobbed.

Alex shut his eyes and took deep breaths.

On the backs of his lids, all he could see was long, thick, copper-colored hair. Pale, smooth skin. Lips that were naturally tinted pink. Eyes that were a soft green, like sea glass.

His poor, miserable, beaten-up body started to crank over, like an old engine wheezing to life. In spite of the fact that he was pumped full of drugs, and hung over, and in pain, warmth spread under his skin.

Feeling something, anything, other than suffering should have been a relief. Instead, the flush kicked up regrets that almost had him crying out.

Reese may be dead, but in Alex's mind, Cassandra was still very much the man's wife. And she always would be.

Chapter Two

The following afternoon Cassandra scanned the small crowd that had gathered in the living room for Gray and Joy's marriage ceremony. Gray's father, still recovering from a stroke, was sitting in a cushioned chair. Nate Walker, who was married to Alex's sister Frankie, was standing against some windows. Next to him was a handsome, black-haired guy with a tattoo on his neck. Spike? Yes, that was his name. Libby, Gray's housekeeper, was behind Spike. In her hands, she had the leash of a golden retriever who had a ring of flowers around his neck.

At the head of the room, in front of the fire, there was a collared minister holding a leather book. Flanking him were Gray and his best man, Sean O'Banyon, as well as Alex's two sisters, Joy and Frankie.

As Cass caught Gray's eye and waved to him, she thought the man had never looked happier. She'd known him for almost a decade and had watched him grow so hard she'd worried that no one could reach him. But here he was, smiling like a schoolboy, love shining in his eyes as he shifted his weight impatiently.

Cass went over and stood next to the dog. Spike was stroking one of the retriever's ears, and the man flashed her a smile, his odd yellow eyes crinkling at the corners.

"You want to take Ernest's other side?" he said quietly, as if he sensed she was nervous.

The dog looked up, clearly seconding the invitation.

She laid a hand on Ernest's soft head. While patting, she glanced behind her.

"Don't worry," Libby whispered. "I just left Joy in the kitchen. She hasn't forgotten what she's supposed to do in that gown."

But the bride wasn't who Cass was looking for.

Moments later the double doors from the dining room opened and Joy appeared. Dressed in a simple white satin sheath, and holding a small bouquet of cream-colored roses, she walked up to Gray, glowing like a sunrise.

Cass glanced over her shoulder once more. She'd been steeling herself to see Alex all morning, sure that he wouldn't miss his sister's wedding. He was in rough shape, but certainly not that rough.

Although, it wasn't as if she were going to volunteer to check on him.

Just as the minister flipped open the *Book of Common Prayer,* she caught a movement over to the right.

Cass's eyes grabbed and held on to Alex as he came in on crutches. He positioned himself in the far corner, leaning back against the wall and kicking out his cast. He'd shaved, and his damp hair was brushed straight back from his forehead. Without any whiskers or bangs, the bones in his face were very clear. His high, carved cheekbones. That hard jawline. The straight nose.

He was wearing a different pair of flannel pajama bottoms, in a Black Watch plaid. One of the legs had been split up the side to accommodate his cast and a couple of safety pins had been used to keep the two halves together above his knee. His button-down shirt was white and pressed, tucked neatly into the waistband.

His eyes were trained on the ceremony. Which was good because she didn't want to get caught staring at him.

She forced herself to look away.

Alex knew the moment Cassandra's gaze left him. It was a goddamned relief.

And he did a good job of not staring at her. He kept his head forward, staying focused on his sister.

At least until the minister addressed Gray. "Will you love her and comfort her, honor and keep her…"

Alex shifted his head a little to the left so he could catch sight of Cassandra in his peripheral vision. She was wearing a spectacular dark red jacket-and-skirt combo that fit her body as if made for it. Which the clothes undoubtedly had been.

But it wasn't the fancy threads that made her beautiful. She was bent to the side in her high heels, stroking the dog's head. Little blond hairs were getting all over the beautiful suit but she didn't care. She just urged Ernest closer, smiling at him as he leaned into her.

Will you love her…

I will, he thought. All the days of my worthless life.

And he wanted to comfort her. He just couldn't do that

without dishonoring her and his dead friend. Not knowing how he felt. Knowing what he'd done.

"I will," Gray said from up front.

After the bride and groom kissed, the couple turned and faced the small assembly. As Joy's happy eyes met Alex's, he was glad he'd come down. He nodded at her, gave her a smile and then propped his weight on the crutches. He wasn't going to stay for the reception and wanted to leave before he got trapped talking to people.

As he made his way out into the hall, he looked up at the grand front staircase. Three flights, two landings. Probably forty or so steps. It was going to take him a good ten minutes to get up them.

"Yo, you need help?" Spike asked casually. The guy had obviously followed him out at a discreet distance.

Spike was a good guy, Alex thought. Calm, steady, even though he looked like a dangerous criminal with the tattoos and piercings. He and Nate were partners in the White Caps kitchen and had catered the wedding at Gray's house.

"Thanks, man, but I'm good."

Alex started for the rear of the house. Taking the back stairs to the second floor was better. That way, no one would watch him struggle.

As he pushed open the kitchen's swinging door, he noticed the place smelled fantastic and was surprised when his stomach checked in with a faded version of hunger pangs. Punching the crutches into the floor and swinging his body along, he paused when he heard his name called out.

He smiled as he looked back at Joy. "Hey, married woman."

"Thank you so much for coming down." She ran over and threw her arms around his neck, holding on so tightly he could barely breathe. Unable to return the embrace because of the crutches, he dropped his head down to his sister's shoulder. He was a little shaken by how much his presence seemed to mean to her.

"Thank you," she whispered again.

"Wouldn't have missed it for the world."

There was the sound of laughter and then the flap door was thrown open.

Gray's best man came barreling into the kitchen. With his arm around Cassandra.

The Wall Street big shot was laughing and smiling. "—so Spike and Nate deserve a break, you and I are it, baby cakes."

The two pulled up short. And Alex found himself measuring the guy for a fight.

Which was insane.

First of all, Cassandra was allowed to have anyone she wanted touch her.

Secondly, that slick bastard may have been in a suit, but as soon as O'Banyon registered Alex's expression, he shifted his stance and brought up his free hand as if on reflex. Like he'd been in quite a few physical altercations and had no problem being in another one.

Now ordinarily, Alex wouldn't have been put off at all by a worthy opponent. Except he knew damn well he'd have trouble taking on anything bigger than a field mouse in his current condition.

And for God's sake, it was his sister's wedding day.

Joy, bless her heart, seemed clueless about the aggression swirling around her. "Alex, have you met Sean O'Banyon? He's one of Gray's best friends."

The man dropped his arm from Cassandra's body, offering the palm that had just been on the top of her hips.

Yeah, right, Alex thought.

"You understand if I don't shake," he said, smiling with his lips, but not his eyes.

O'Banyon nodded once, keeping his gaze steady as he dropped his arm. Cassandra looked back and forth between them, as if measuring the antagonism and being confused by it.

Abruptly Joy stepped in front of Alex as if she were trying to distract him. Maybe his little sister did know what was up, after all.

"Would you like me to bring you something to eat?"

"No. It's your wedding reception. You stay with your husband." Alex looked across the room and spoke before his brain could shut his mouth. "Cassandra will run something up. Won't you. Baby cakes."

Cassandra frowned. "Of course."

Alex hobbled over to the stairs, aware that he was going to be the topic of conversation the moment he was out of earshot. Not that he gave a damn.

As he braced for the ascent, he cursed himself.

The idea was to keep that woman away from him. Why was he paving her way to his bedroom?

Because, his inner idiot pointed out, at least if she were upstairs with him, she wouldn't be in the arms of that pale-eyed, slick-suited, flashy bastard.

Alex pegged the crutches into the first step and pushed himself up.

Damn it. He should have taken the front stairs when he'd had the chance.

* * *

Cass heard the kitchen door swing shut as Joy went back to the party. She also registered the sounds of people moving around in the dining room on the other side: footsteps, talking, laughter, a bottle of wine being uncorked with a pop.

But what she listened to were the grunts and thudding as Alex dragged himself upstairs.

"So that's Alex Moorehouse," Sean drawled. "*The* Alex Moorehouse. I've read about him. Won the America's Cup how many times?"

Cass tried to remember what she was doing in the kitchen. "We're bringing in the food," she murmured.

Sean flashed her an odd look. "Yes, we are."

She went over to the massive Viking stove and started cracking the doors on the different ovens. There were so many covered dishes warming, she wondered where to start.

"Not exactly the friendly type, is he?" Sean said, leaning against a counter. "Even busted up like that, he was ready to ring my head like a bell."

Sean didn't seem offended in the slightest, though why would he be? Given the way O'Banyon lived his life, he was probably most at ease around hard-core men like himself, especially if things were getting aggressive. Wall Street just hadn't managed to tame the South Boston street thug he'd once been.

"Was he always like that?" Sean prompted.

"He's been through a lot." Using a pair of folded dish towels, she drew out a roast beef that rested on a spectacular Royal Crown Derby platter. Her arms strained and she hoped she wouldn't drop the thing. The plate was worth more than the stove.

"I'll take that," Sean said, relieving her of the load like it didn't weigh more than a potholder.

Working in tandem, the two of them brought in covered dishes of wild rice and minted peas and broccoli au gratin and pearl onions. By the time everyone had drifted in from the living room, the buffet was set up. Cass let the others go through the line first. When the other guests were all sitting down and eating, she picked up a gold-rimmed plate and a damask napkin roll.

She tried to imagine what Alex would want to eat. Did he like his roast beef from the pink center or the more well-done edges? And how much rice? Would he want gravy? When she passed by the basket of freshly made rolls, she put one on the side and then thought of how thin he was. She added another and put a big slab of butter next to them.

"I'll be right back," she said to no one in particular.

Silence sucked the party sounds out of the room as every person at the table stopped eating and talking and just watched her go. As if she were heading into a lion's den.

Why did he pick me? she wondered.

Unless he enjoyed torturing her.

As she walked upstairs, she was anxious even though she told herself to stop making such a big deal about it all. He was just a man. Just another human being.

She paused in front of his door.

No, he wasn't, she thought. There was something about Alex that was different, and she'd recognized it the moment she'd first met him. He was raw and wild where other men were tame and bland.

No wonder he was drawn to the sea. It was probably the only thing on the planet big and mean enough to challenge him.

She thought about her husband. Reese had loved sailing, but he'd had a thriving business and a home life he'd enjoyed. Though he'd be gone a week at a time or sometimes even more, he'd always returned to her and been glad to be off the yacht. Alex had never stopped. She'd heard that he was on land maybe only four or five weeks a year. The rest of the time he was captaining boats, training crews, fighting the ocean and his competitors to win.

The past three months must have felt like a prison to him, she thought.

"I can't eat if the food's in the hall," Alex said from inside the room.

Cass jumped. Taking a deep breath, she balanced the plate on one hand and opened the door. "How did you know I was—"

"The smell."

She looked around the room to avoid meeting his eyes. "Where do you want this?"

"Here." He made space on his bedside table by pushing pill bottles and an empty glass to the side.

"I—ah, I didn't know what you liked. So I brought you a little bit of everything." She put the plate and the napkin roll down. "Do you want me to get you some water?"

"Thanks."

She picked up the glass and went for the bathroom. At the sink, she ran the water until it was cold under her fingertips and then filled the tumbler up. When she came back, she noticed he hadn't touched the food.

She looked at him. His eyes were hooded as he watched her every movement.

"You should eat it while it's hot." She put the glass down.

"Probably." He shifted his head, regarding her with disarming stillness. "So how well do you know that guy?"

"Who?"

"O'Banyon. Wasn't that his name?"

Talk about out of left field, she thought.

"I, ah, I know him fairly well. He was Reese's investment banker, but he's also a dear friend of Gray's. They went to school together." She frowned. "Are you going to eat?"

"You sound like my sisters." But he picked up the napkin, unwrapped the heavy silver and leaned to one side, considering what was on the plate.

He looked about as enthused as someone facing a traffic jam.

After dropping a couple of peas on the way to his mouth, and struggling to cut up the meat, he leaned back against the pillow. He wasn't giving up, she thought. Just bored and uninterested.

"Here, let me help you." She snatched the fork from his hand.

"I don't need—"

Ignoring him, she sat down on the mattress and put the plate in her lap. With a low groan, he deliberately moved his body away. Even though it made him wince.

Trying to ignore his aversion, she made busy work cutting up the roast. Then she loaded the fork and faced off with him.

He glared at her, lips pressed tight.

"Open your mouth," she said.

"I'm not a child."

"Then prove it. Accept the help you need and eat."

Oh, man, he was pissed off. His body was practically vibrating.

But he did what she asked. And as soon as the fork was clean, she piled it high again.

On the fourth trip to his mouth, she made a mistake. She watched his lips as they parted. Watched the bright white of his front teeth clamp down on the silver. Watched the fork emerge, empty. She saw his jaw working as he chewed, the hollows under his cheekbones undulating. Then his Adam's apple slid up and down in his throat as he swallowed.

She became curiously aware of the width of his shoulders. Of the thick cords of muscle that ran up his neck. Of the way his hair curled over the collar of his shirt.

"Cassandra," he snapped. As if he'd said her name more than once.

Startled, she looked at his face. His eyes were cold.

"I said, that's enough. I'll take it from here."

He grabbed the fork and the plate.

Cass got off the bed. "I'll be back for the dishes."

"Don't bother."

"It's no—"

"Besides, I'm sure you'll be otherwise occupied at the end of the night."

"What?"

"Does O'Banyon like to get babied? You cut up his meat for him, too? Mommy love ain't a turn-on for me, but hey, every man's different, right?"

It was hard to know whether his tone or his words were more insulting, she thought.

She opened her mouth, but he cut her off.

"Before you tell me I'm a bastard, I already know that. And if you're thinking of branching out from there, I've had bigger, tougher and more creative *sailors* take a run at my hide. You're going to have to do a real stand-up job with the curses to come up with anything fresh, sweetheart. Oh, I'm sorry, it's baby cakes, isn't it?"

His eyes raked over her with such complete dismissal, she felt as though she was mostly invisible but that what little he saw of her, he despised.

He laughed at her silence. "Not even going to take a try at it? Good call. Because there's absolutely nothing you can say to me that'll be a news flash."

She brushed her hair back, hand trembling. In the space of a minute, he'd driven her to the brink of tears. Again.

"I just don't understand why I'm so repulsive to you," she whispered. "I don't know what I've done to deserve—"

She stopped. Showing more vulnerability was not a smart move.

Cass turned away as the first humiliating tear got stuck in her lashes.

Damn it, she was *not* going to cry in front of him.

As she bolted across the room, the curse he let out was low and vile.

"Cassandra."

She grabbed for the door.

"Cassandra."

When she heard a flurry of activity on the bed and something hit the floor, she looked over her shoulder.

Alex was upright and wildly off balance, trying to lurch toward her after having dropped the crutch. If he went much farther, he was going to fall on his face. She rushed back for him.

Chapter Three

Alex had a feeling he was headed for the floor, but he didn't care.

Man, he'd been wrong. She *had* surprised him. Her soft, sad words had ripped through his chest.

As he tumbled forward into thin air, she lunged for him. But the moment before her body met his, he pushed her aside and threw his arms out, bracing himself for impact. Going solo for the thin oriental rug was a no-brainer.

Because however hard the floor was going to be, knowing how she felt against him would be harder.

He took the brunt of the fall on his right shoulder. By some blessing, his fragile leg was spared, though his other knee got twisted in the process. As he rolled over onto his back with a nasty curse, he saw he'd thrown her on the bed. He caught a gorgeous flash of her calf and thigh before she rearranged her skirt and stood up.

He knew damn well he'd better get going with the apology. She was on the express train out of his room and who could blame her?

"I'm sorry," he said roughly.

She glanced down at him. Her eyes were too shiny.

Ah, hell, he'd made her cry.

"I'm damn sorry."

There was no real reaction, just a shift of her shoulders. "I'd offer to help you up, but I know you won't let me."

"Cassandra, I—" He banged his head back against the floor in frustration. "I'm sorry I hurt your feelings. And you don't...repulse me."

Her laugh was a travesty. Which made sense because in a way, so was his apology. But what was he supposed to say?

I want you until I hurt. Until I sweat.

I love you with a raw, bleeding need that I've never understood.

And all I know for sure is that you can never be mine.

"I don't repulse you," she repeated slowly. "Is that why you'd rather fall down than have me touch you? God, you are the only person in my adult life who's ever made me feel dirty."

He cursed again. "That's not—"

"Please." She held her hand out and moved away. "Please, don't say anything else. I don't think I can bear any more of your apology. It's worse than your insults."

"Damn it, come here," he commanded.

Her eyes flared. "Screw you."

When she made a move to step over him, he grabbed her ankle, holding her tight. "Come. Down. Here."

"Go. To. Hell."

"Cassandra...please."

She put her hands on her hips and leaned over, her hair falling forward. As he breathed in, he could smell the herbal shampoo she used.

The scent dragged him right back to the one sailing jaunt he'd taken with her and Reese years ago. Reese had insisted that Alex come along, and it had been clear that the man had hoped to get his wife and his best friend on better terms. That trip had been hell. They were supposed to have been gone for five days. Alex had left the boat after two, hopping off at the first port they'd come to.

He'd tried so hard to find fault with her. He'd been desperate to latch on to annoying habits, turns of phrases that irritated him, small rudenesses that proved she wasn't even close to the image of perfection he'd created in his mind. Instead, he'd gotten to know the different shades of her laughter. Her offbeat sense of humor. Her capacity to savor the sun setting into the ocean with the same sad reverence that beat in his own chest.

And being in close quarters with her had made him mental. Every time he'd taken a shower, he'd smelled her shampoo as if the stuff had saturated the air just to mock him. He hadn't been able to use the bar of soap at all because he knew it had been over her skin.

The nights had been…unbearable.

But all that was before she'd walked in and seen him naked. Or rather, he'd come out of the head after a shower, assuming she and Reese were off the boat swimming. He'd heard the sound of indrawn breath and looked over his shoulder. She'd been in the galley kitchen pouring lemonade, and the glass and the pitcher had come unconnected as she'd stared at him. The sound of splashing liquid had been loud in the silence.

He'd covered himself with a towel and leaped back into the head. Gathering himself over the little sink, he'd thanked God that she'd only seen the back of him. Because the front had grown hard and heavy the instant he'd felt her eyes on him.

He'd left the boat within the hour.

Now, as he breathed in again and the scent of her hair tunneled into his nose, he wanted to pull her down on top of him and bury his face in those copper waves. He wanted one of her thighs on either side of his hips. He wanted that skirt of hers up around her waist. He wanted—

"Let go of me," she said tightly.

"No. Come closer." He paused and tacked on, "Please."

He hoped the word would work its magic once again.

As she slowly dropped to her knees, she seemed more confused than angry. He wanted to reach out and take her hand in his. He didn't dare.

"Look, Cassandra, I've spent too much time on the sea with ex-frat boys who are past civil redemption. And my social skills were in the crapper before all that. My temper's always been sharp, but lately I've been god-awful to be around. I shouldn't have asked you to come up here." He cleared his throat. "So I really am sorry."

Her clear, green eyes traced over his face. Such intelligent eyes, he thought. Such warm eyes, though their color was pale.

Gradually the tension left her forehead and her mouth, and she stopped blinking so much.

"You can make it up to me."

"How?" he asked.

"Tell me about your leg. Is it healing?"

Even though the last thing in the world he wanted to talk about was his injury, he figured he owed her an answer.

"No. It's not getting better. They took out the bone and put in a titanium rod. The damn thing didn't take, so they installed a different kind six weeks ago. I'll find out on Monday what happens next."

"What if it didn't work again?"

"Then I'm out of options."

"Out of—" She covered her beautiful mouth with a hand. The pinkie trembled against her jawline. "Oh, Alex."

He shook his head. "Don't worry about it. No matter what happens, I'll deal with it. It's fine."

And no more than he deserved for letting a fine man die. *Her* man die.

He thrust his palms into the floor and pushed his torso upright.

"Will you let me help you up?" she asked.

"No. But you can bring me my crutch."

He hated the idea of hauling himself off the floor in front of her and was grateful when she didn't stare. After he was back on the bed, he shut his eyes, suddenly exhausted.

He heard her moving across the room, toward the door.

"Please finish the food. It will help you heal," she said softly. When he didn't reply, she pressed. "I'll be back to pick that plate up. I'm hoping it will be clean."

The door opened and shut.

Dimly he became aware that his leg was throbbing to the beat of his heart. He waited to see if the shooting agony would go away. The pain got worse.

He knew what that meant. It was going to be a long night.

Alex looked over at his collection of prescription bottles. Reaching past the antibiotics and the anticoagulants and all the other horse pills his doctors wanted him to suck back, he zeroed in on the pain meds. He hated taking the damn things because they put him out, but after that fall, he knew he was going to pay for the hard impact. Popping open the vial, he took two of the knockout specials and then eyed the food.

With a groan, he leaned down toward the floor. And picked up the scotch bottle.

As he unscrewed the top and caught a whiff of oblivion, he thought of Cassandra.

Then looked back over at the plate she'd brought him.

Goddamn it, he was not going to feel guilty because he wanted to get good and wasted. There was nothing wrong about seeking the simple darkness of rest, as opposed to the twisted torture of nightmares.

Okay, so the alcohol didn't really work. At least not for very long. Somehow the hell of the storm always managed to fight through the scotch fog, chewing him up and spitting him out shaky and sweaty and sick to his stomach.

But the brown stuff did get him a couple hours of sleep.

He brought the mouth of the bottle to his lips. And found his eyes on the plate of food again.

"Is everything all right up there?" Gray asked as Cass walked into the dining room. "We heard something hit the floor. Something big."

"Everything's fine."

Her friend narrowed his shrewd eyes but let the subject drop.

Cass got some food and headed for the empty seat next to Sean. The man stood up and pulled out her chair.

"Did I tell you I spoke with Mick Rhodes?" Sean asked

as he pushed the seat in under her. "He loves what you did to his place in Greenwich. Thinks you're an architectural genius as well as one hell of a general contractor."

She smiled, thinking of Rhodes and the antique, six-bedroom Colonial in Greenwich he loved so much. Some people had great love for their houses and he was one of them. The man had been like a mother hen with a chick.

"He was a prince to work for."

Sean eyed her dryly. "We talking about the same guy? Because Rhodes has been described as a lot of things. Prince usually isn't one of them."

"He was fine with me. We had a lot of fun together on that project."

"Amazing," Sean muttered as he picked up his wine-glass and leaned back in the chair. "So I've been meaning to ask you, what kind of projects are you doing now?"

"I haven't been working much since—" she cleared her throat "—since Reese died."

She felt a strong hand on her shoulder and glanced over at O'Banyon's hard face. His gray eyes were always flinty, even when he was in a good mood, but at this moment, they were as close to warm as ice could get.

"How you been doing?" he asked quietly, his Boston accent bleeding into the words.

"Better than I thought." She smiled. "We were great friends, he and I. Even today I caught myself reaching for the cell phone. I was down by the lake. The waves were choppy and gray and the sky was milky white and the mountains were almost purple, and I thought, I need to call Reese and tell him what this looks like."

She stared down at her food. Her appetite was gone and she thought of Alex, upstairs. No wonder he had no interest in eating. He'd lost his best friend, his partner. He'd been through multiple operations. And he was now facing the possible amputation of a leg.

"Anything I can do?" Sean said.

She covered his hand with her own. "I'll get through this. And work's going to help. In fact, I'd love to find a project I could totally sink into. I think I'm ready."

"Are you truly looking for something to do?" Joy asked gently from the head of the table.

Cass smiled at the younger woman who had become a friend. "Yes."

"Would you be willing to take a look at White Caps?"

"Your family's house?"

Joy nodded. "We'd like to try and repair the fire damage quickly so we can reopen for next season in June. We just don't know where to start. Or who to trust."

"You run a B and B out of the mansion, don't you?"

"Yes. That's why we want to move fast."

Cass thought about it for a moment. "We could go tomorrow morning before Sean and I leave for the city."

"That would be wonderful. I didn't want to ask you, but we'd really appreciate your guidance."

"How much did the fire take?"

"The kitchen and the staff quarters got the worst of it, but two guest bedrooms were damaged as well. Fortunately, the insurance company is going to pay up."

"Well…I'd love to take a look at it."

When dinner was over, Cass helped Libby clean up in the kitchen. By the time they were finished, all the guests had turned in for the night. As Cass headed upstairs, she told herself there was no reason to go back to Alex's room.

She was arguing with herself when she realized she was standing in front of his door.

Slowly turning the knob, she put her head in. In the glow from the bedside lamp, she saw that he was still lying on top of the covers. There was a book facedown in his lap and his eyes were squeezed shut. Although he might have technically been asleep, considering the tension in his face, he was not resting.

Stepping inside, she shut the door so light from the outside hall wouldn't wake him up. She was very quiet as she walked through the dim room, focusing only on the man stretched out so immense and motionless on the bed. When her foot knocked into something, she looked down. It was a scotch bottle that was mostly empty. As she righted the thing, she glanced at the prescription pills by the lamp. She recognized some of the names. They were big-league painkillers.

She watched his breathing. It was very slow.

What if he'd mixed the drugs with alcohol?

She glanced at the plate. At least he'd eaten most of the food she'd brought him.

"Alex?" she said softly.

She touched his forearm. His skin was warm.

"Alex?"

Bending down, she took a sniff through her nose. She couldn't detect any liquor smell at all, and his breathing was regular.

He's fine, she thought. Just asleep. So pick up that plate and leave the poor man alone.

Instead, she stared down at his face, thinking about the way he'd lashed out at her and then apologized with such rough honesty.

On a crazy impulse she put her hand out and touched his cheek.

She immediately reeled her arm back in. Boy, he'd have tossed her out on her ass if he'd been awake.

But he wasn't. And the hard lines of his face drew her like nothing ever had.

She reached out again.

Alex came awake the moment something brushed over his cheek, but he didn't move, didn't open his eyes. He couldn't tell whether he was dreaming or not.

Then the touch came back. This time on the side of his jaw.

He breathed deeply, trying to rouse himself to consciousness, but when he caught the scent of herbs, he stopped the fight. He took in another lungful of air just to be sure.

When the smell of rosemary came again, he wanted to weep. His dreams, so horrible, so cruel, had finally brought Cassandra to him.

He shifted his head, trying to get closer to her touch.

"It's you, Miracle," he whispered. "It's truly you...."

The touch disappeared. He made a sound of protest in his throat. He couldn't have her in the real world, couldn't bear the shame of betraying his best friend. But in this dream she could be his. At least for a small while. At least in a small way.

"Please," he begged softly, raggedly. "Please, just once more. Touch me."

When he felt the sensation return, this time there was more of it, as if she'd laid her palm against his face. He nuzzled her soft hand, rubbing his skin against hers. Then he kissed the pad of her thumb.

He heard an indrawn breath. Not his own.

Alex didn't think twice about what he did next. In this

twilight fantasy, he could be free with the woman he loved. He could know her touch and she could know his and it would be all right. Because dreams weren't real.

He took her hand and drew it down the side of his throat, until it was under the collar of his shirt. He moved her palm back and forth, stroking himself with her flesh, relishing the knowledge that it was her.

In a wicked rush, he wanted to feel her touch all over him. And he wanted to touch her. With his hands. His mouth. His whole body.

He shifted his head back, pushing his neck up into her caress. His shirt was blocking her access so he popped the buttons free, wondering dimly why in his dream he wasn't naked.

There was a gasp as he took her hand and moved it down his chest. Had he made the sound? Maybe.

Except as he was taking her touch over his stomach, the swift inhale came again and he thought, no, that wasn't him. It was her. And the sound told him she liked what his shirt had revealed, that she liked touching him.

But then why did her hand resist when he got to the waistband of his pajama bottoms? Abruptly he became aware of a weight at his hips. A book, he thought. There was a book on top of his hot erection.

Man, he was going to have to work on his fantasies. Clothes. Books. For God's sake, he should make it easier on them.

He let go of her hand and pushed the hardcover off his body. Arching his back and carrying the movement into his hips, he wanted her to see what her touch did to him. How ready he was for her. And he was hoping that she'd stroke him there. Where he ached for her so badly.

There was a hiss. Followed by something close to a groan.

Alex arched for her again, confused when she still hesitated. He could hear the sex in her voice, the feminine need. And her palm remained on his stomach, her touch like sunlight. She just wasn't moving.

So he placed his hand over hers and guided her lower. Then lower still.

The moment she made contact with his hard length, the groan was his, the hoarse words pumping through the thick air. He'd meant the intimacy to be just a beginning for them, but his body had different ideas. A mighty release came up on him, fast and hot as lightning, hovering just on the edge of his control. He breathed in harshly, smelled rosemary and moved his hips against her palm.

In an answer to his prayers, her fingers gripped him through the flannel and that was all it took. Ecstasy spilled out of him in surges that racked his body. Carried away, soaring high, shattered and made whole in the same instant, he uttered three words in a voice that cracked from the burden of his long-kept secret.

"I love you...."

The relief of finally speaking the truth ushered in the peace that came as he drifted back into his body.

And it was okay. Here, in his dream, it was all right to let his feelings out. There was no terrible dishonor, no sense of disloyalty. Just a simple truth that had burned him to his soul from the moment he had first seen her.

Darkness reached up and embraced him, pulling him under.

For the first time since the storm the nightmares didn't come.

Chapter Four

Cass headed to her room on legs that felt really unreliable. Shutting her door, she sagged back against the panels.

She wasn't sure what shocked her most. What had just happened. Or what Alex had said.

She put her face in her hands. With shocking clarity, she could still hear him crying out. Could picture his body going rigid and then trembling from shock waves until he fell still.

She'd never actually watched a man…well, do *that*. At least not in that way. Not with that kind of sensual abandon.

She certainly hadn't meant for things to go that far. From the moment he'd slipped her hand under his shirt, she'd told herself to pull back. But the more she felt of him, the more she heard him speak, the more she watched his body move on that bed, the less able she'd been to turn away. His response to her had been unbelievable, as if he'd waited for years just for her touch. As if he were desperate for the smallest crumbs of her attention.

Except he hadn't been dreaming of her, Cass told herself. He didn't ache for her. He didn't even *like* her.

Though, at the time, she'd almost believed he'd known whose hands were touching him. She'd been convinced that she was the one he needed so badly when it had been happening.

Or maybe she'd just wanted to be that woman to him.

Now, there was a thought she wasn't going to dwell on.

Squeezing her eyes shut, she tried to find some equilibrium. Instead, all she saw was Alex's muscular chest and ribbed stomach…and his bold, demanding erection as it strained against soft flannel. He'd been hot and hard and thick under her hand, and his response to her touch had been explosive. Beyond erotic. She'd gripped him and then he'd moved his hips in a sinuous thrust. His breath had broken. And she'd felt the flesh under her hand jerk and…

"Oh, do yourself a favor and stop going there," she muttered.

Then he'd spoken those words.

I love you.

Who did he love? she wondered with a strange ache in her chest. What kind of woman had gotten under that hard surface to the man beneath?

Well, whoever she was, she must be extraordinary. She'd have to be. Because someone like him, someone with such high standards, would only love a woman who was flat-out amazing.

And he *really* loved that lady, with feelings as strong and powerful as the body he lived in. His heartfelt yearning had cracked his voice. All that desire had ripped through him at the mere touch of a hand.

He *burned* for his woman.

Cass walked into the bathroom and thought of Reese.

She'd respected her husband like no one else. Had valued him as a friend and a business advisor. And she'd owed him a debt she could never have repaid.

But she couldn't say that she'd ever loved him. At least not the way Alex loved his Miracle woman.

Picking up her toothbrush, she popped the flip top on a tube of Crest and tried to keep the ribbon of chalky blue on the white bristles.

As she brushed, she focused on the past instead of the present. She'd married Reese because he'd asked her and because she'd wanted to, even though he'd been twenty years older than she was and she was to be his third wife. She'd always yearned for a family and a home and a place to feel safe after a childhood of fear and instability. She'd been sure that Reese would always protect her. Would always support her.

Even when he strayed.

She'd suspected he might, eventually. Reese had been a great admirer of beautiful things, and his aggressive nature had driven him to acquire whatever caught his eye. Companies. Art. Jewels. Boats. Houses.

Women.

She'd known what she was getting into when she'd walked down the aisle with him, so what had happened later hadn't been a big surprise. He'd been discreet about the affairs and it had taken her a while to learn the truth. And when she'd known for sure? She hadn't confronted him, she'd just kept on going like nothing was wrong.

The reasons she'd had then for staying quiet were ones she didn't understand now.

Maybe it had just been because…she hadn't cared as much as she should have.

She missed Reese. She mourned him. She wished she'd conceived the child they had tried for.

But she had never loved him down to her soul.

She thought of Alex again.

What would it be like to have a man who cared that much? she wondered. Who wanted you and only you. Who could see no other woman in a room, who could not imagine holding another female in his arms.

That must be something, she thought, rinsing her mouth out. That must really be something.

Alex woke up late in the morning with an uneasy feeling. That dream. That sensual, shattering dream.

He looked down. His shirt was open and pushed off his chest. The book was buried in the comforter at his side. And he needed a quick shower.

His heart started pounding. Had it been real? Had she come to him?

What the hell had come out of his mouth?

Dread pooled in his gut, but then he looked over and saw the plate. Maybe she hadn't been in his room after all.

Calm down, he told himself. She wasn't here except in your mind. You've wanted that woman for a long time, and she's in the bedroom down the hall. Of course your subconscious is going to kick something to the surface.

Levering himself up and off the bed, he went carefully to the bathroom where he showered with a plastic bag tied around his leg and then shaved. He was surprised that it felt good to be up and moving around for once, so he decided to head to the kitchen for some breakfast. Fortunately, it sounded as if the coast was clear. The house was quiet and he figured he'd somehow managed to sleep through all the early-morning departures of the guests.

Which meant Cassandra would be gone, as well.

This was good, he told himself.

He pulled on a different set of split pajama bottoms, a worn T-shirt from a Boston Marathon he'd run in years ago and a black fleece. As he went out into the hall, he looked both ways as if it were a busy street. The last thing he needed was to step into someone's path. He was about as stable as a two-legged table.

Come to think of it, where was the dog? He loved Ernest, but that golden retriever could knock him on his ass in a heartbeat, and muzzle-to-mouth resuscitation was not a treatment option he was looking to explore.

Alex started for the back stairs but changed his mind. The front ones were slightly deeper and could accommodate his feet better. It took him a good ten minutes to actually make it to the first floor, but he felt stupidly pleased with the effort.

Then he thought about his T-shirt. Running 26.2 miles in two and a half hours used to be something he took pride in. Now getting to the kitchen was a big, fat, hairy deal.

Damn, he was pathetic.

He went into the dining room and braced the swinging door in place so it couldn't open.

"Libby? You in there?" he called out.

"Alex! Are you okay?" The housekeeper sounded worried.

"Grab hold of your boy, will you? I'm coming in."

"Done."

Alex pushed open the door and was greeted by whines of affection and a mad, impotent scampering of dog feet. While Libby held Ernest in place, Alex came over and stroked the dog into a relative calm.

"Would you like some breakfast?" the older woman asked. "I can make you some of the dry toast you like."

He looked up. Her lovely, worn face was so hopeful, he was tempted to put in a special request.

"Actually, I—" He cleared his throat. He didn't like being waited on, but he had a feeling this flash of energy he was sporting wasn't going to last long. "I'd like some pancakes. With butter and syrup. And bacon. I want bacon. Coffee, too."

God, he was hungry. For the first time in so long, he was dying for some food.

Libby's eyes flared. "Go sit down at the table. I'll make it right away."

As he settled into a chair, Ernest snuggled up close, leaning against his good leg.

"Do you take sugar?" Libby asked.

The question made him realize he hadn't asked for any coffee since he'd come to the mansion.

Hell, how long *had* it been since he'd had a normal breakfast? Sitting up at a table. Like a real person.

"I like it black, thanks."

"It'll be ready in a second. This pot's almost finished brewing."

While he watched the woman bustle around, he wished he could help and felt badly that all the activity was just about him.

"Hey, Libby, maybe I'll scratch that big order," he said. "A little cereal would be great. I don't want you going to—"

"Alex Moorehouse, you shut your mouth. And I don't want it open again until you're putting a fork in it."

He had to smile. There weren't a lot of people who put him in his place on or off the water. Wouldn't his crew get a kick out of the fact that one of the short-listers was a white-haired grandmother.

Libby brought the coffee over first, and Alex closed his eyes as he took the first sip. The stuff was steaming hot and strong enough to wake the dead.

In a word, divine.

When he started to sweat, he realized he was sitting in a shaft of sunlight. He peeled off the fleece and went back to work on the mug.

As he sipped and stroked Ernest's ear, the moment sank into him with the pleasurable flush of an unexpected kind word. The dog's head was a warm weight on his good leg. Libby's friendly chatter about Saranac Lake's characters was like the crackle of a cheery fire. The rhythmic hiss of a wire whisk cutting through batter reminded him of happy mornings from his childhood.

He settled back against the chair and closed his eyes again. His leg was throbbing, but it was a dull pump, not the kind of pain that made his skin ache. He took a deep breath and felt his shoulders loosen on the exhale.

"More coffee?" Libby asked gently.

He opened his lids and smiled. "Please."

She brought over the coffeepot, refilled his mug to the brim and then hurried back to the griddle to flip over the pancakes. When the bacon slices hit the pan, he shut his eyes once more.

Hunger cut through him and he welcomed it.

Minutes later Libby set a heavy plate in front of him

along with a stick of butter and a gravy boat full of syrup. He put a slice of bacon in his mouth while he lathered up the pancakes and doused them in maple heaven. Then he tore through the food.

When he put his fork down, he and Libby were both a little surprised at the clean plate. Ernest looked disappointed.

"You want more?" Libby asked.

Alex rubbed his belly. "Ah, yeah. Thanks."

As a cold November wind gusted up from the lake, Cassandra put her hands on her hips and surveyed the ruins of the White Caps Bed and Breakfast. When she stepped toward the house, she heard the five people behind her move along like a small herd. Frankie and Nate, Joy, Gray and Sean had all come for the tour.

Wow, what a house this is, she thought, measuring the structure's superb, Federal lines. Sitting regally on a bluff that jutted out into the lake, the place was a real charmer, all white clapboards and shiny black shutters. The fire damage in the back was jarring, like a bruise on the face of a beautiful woman.

"Thomas Crane was the architect, right?" she asked as she walked over to the kitchen where the destruction was the most severe.

"It was one of Crane's last commissions," Frankie replied.

"Do you have the original plans?"

"Fortunately, yes. The set has always been kept out in my father's workshop so it survived the fire."

Cassandra lifted a sheet of thick plastic and stepped through what had been the kitchen door. Even though the fire had been a month ago, the pungent stench of smoke and ash hung in the air.

"This part of the house wasn't added on later, was it?"

"No, it's in the plans," Frankie said. "When our father converted the mansion into a B and B in the seventies, all he did was bring up the kitchen to restaurant code. He didn't make any changes to the structure."

Cass looked around, assessing the load-bearing walls. They seemed mostly solid, though someone had buttressed one with a couple of two-by-fours to make sure it didn't sag. She glanced upward. The ceiling was burnt through in places so she could see past the joists to the second floor.

She pointed over to the scorched back staircase. "I'd like to go upstairs, but not using those."

"The ones in front are safe," Nate replied.

A half hour later, the group was out on the lawn again.

"So what do you think?" Frankie asked as they piled into Sean's massive Mercedes-Benz.

Cass gathered her thoughts before answering. "I'd have to see the plans and reflect a little before I could give you even the roughest estimate of time and cost."

"But you don't think we need to tear the wing down and rebuild it from scratch, right?"

"God, no! Although you will have to go slowly because you should save as much as you can. Given the historic nature of the house, a contractor who has respect for its pedigree will be the best choice for you." Her voice drifted. "I tell you, the workmanship on the moldings in those front rooms is remarkable. The hours of labor… Thank heavens that balustrade going up the main stairs wasn't ruined. You just don't see that kind of curvilinear detail very often. Amazing what the human hand can do with a tool, isn't it?"

She closed her eyes, savoring the images she'd stored up.

What a house.

When they pulled up to Gray's, the group unpacked themselves and went through the back door into the kitchen. From around the corner, Ernest came barreling at them, stopping to greet each of the arrivals like he was the official ambassador of the household.

"So will you do it?" Frankie asked.

"Do what?" Cass replied while taking off her coat and stepping into the kitchen.

"Be our architect and general contractor."

Cass stopped, but not only because of the question. Alex was across the room, sitting at the table.

With a flush, she saw his body arching up under her hand.

She looked down quickly.

Which was actually a good thing. Because she'd just dropped her coat on the dog.

"Well?" Frankie prompted. "We can pay you. The insurance company is going after the manufacturer of the gas stove that started the fire. Money's not going to be a problem."

"I, uh—"

Actually, I'd like to go lie down now. Because being in the same room with your brother this morning is making me dizzy and incoherent.

Sean stepped forward. "Cass, are your bags packed? We gotta hit the road, woman."

She cleared her throat. "Yes. They're in my room."

"I'll get them." As Sean strode through the kitchen, he nodded at Alex. "Moorehouse."

"O'Banyon," Alex shot back.

The sound of the rough, low voice took Cass right back to the man's bedside. Where she'd touched his body. Where she'd watched him move. Where he'd—

Get a *grip*.

Well, she'd sure had one last night....

Cass shut her eyes, wondering if anyone else in the room had noticed the floor was weaving underfoot.

"Cassandra, I saw the way you looked at our house," Frankie said. "You're perfect for this project."

Cass shook herself to attention and sensed Alex's eyes narrowing on her. She had a feeling he wouldn't appreciate her working on his family's home.

"Why don't the three of you talk it over," she hedged. "I'll go back to my office, check in with my partners, see what the schedule looks like. I know you're going to want this project to move fast if you hope to open for the season in—when was it?"

"June," Frankie said. "If you started around the first of December, you'd have seven months."

Sean came back, Vuitton duffel bags and suitcases hanging off him like he was a bellboy.

"I still can't believe how much stuff you pack," he said as he headed to the back door. "Gray, you sure you know what you're in for, signing on for one of these fashion types?"

"I'm buying a trolley," the man said as he tucked his new wife under his arm.

"Good idea. It's either that or a back brace." Sean shot Cass a wink as he went on by. "Now let's do it, beautiful."

The assembled masses filed outside with Ernest leading the way. Libby went with them, no doubt to catch the dog before he tore off.

Cass stayed behind, swallowing through a dry throat.

She couldn't leave without one last look at Alex.

Lifting her eyes, she met his own. They were what she expected. Cool. Remote.

"I hope everything goes well for you tomorrow at the doctor's," she said.

He nodded once. "Thanks."

It's you, Miracle. It's truly you.

Please. Touch me. Just once more.

I love you....

Who is your woman, she thought as she stared at him. And where is she when you're going through this hell? Why are you alone now?

She cleared her throat. "Look, I don't want you to feel awkward about saying no. You know, about me working on your family's house. I wanted to give you an out, which was why I suggested—"

"I'm a big boy. If I don't like something, I'm perfectly capable of letting people know it."

"Oh, of course." As if she needed a reminder that he didn't like women who mothered him.

"Something else on your mind, Cassandra?" he said softly.

The back door opened. Sean put his head inside.

"Yo, Cass. I've got a meeting at Rhodes Lewis this afternoon. We've got to move."

"On a Sunday?" she blurted.

"You know me, twenty-four seven. Come on, woman." The door banged shut.

When she looked back at Alex, she was glad she was leaving. His eyes had turned dangerous.

"Better run along," he drawled. "Your friend's obviously the impatient type."

The word *friend* was pronounced more like *lover*, she thought. And his disapproval would have freeze-dried an open flame.

He obviously thought she was seeing Sean, and that it

was way too soon after Reese's death for her to be with another man, but she wasn't going to waste time correcting the misconception. Given his tight face, she wasn't going to change his mind without working him over with a chisel and a hammer.

"Goodbye, Alex," she whispered.

He said nothing.

As she left the house, she was quite convinced she was never going to see him again.

Somehow the pain of the loss was stunning.

Chapter Five

A month later Alex stared out of the workshop's picture window and measured the milky sky. Snow was coming over the weekend and it wasn't going to be the picturesque, flurry variety. This was going to be a shut-in special, the kind of load that would bring out the county plows that were as big as houses and sounded like thunder when they went by.

God, he loved the north. There was real weather up here.

He shifted his eyes. The lake down below was the color of a dove, mostly gray with paler blushes on the tips of restless waves. The mountains were likewise subdued, their rock faces revealed now that the leaves were off the trees. December wasn't so much dour at Saranac Lake as muted, and he liked the rugged isolation of the place. No tourists, no seasonal fruitcakes. Just the hard-core natives and Mother Nature. Bliss.

He frowned, wondering whether Cassandra would like all the quiet. Probably not. She lived a fast, flashy life in Manhattan, and was always showing up in the *New York Times* style section and *Vanity Fair,* or at least that was what Reese had said. A woman like her wouldn't want to be stuck in a house with a blazing fire and nothing to do but make love and watch the snow fall.

Alex drove his cane into the floor and limped over to the bathroom. On the way, he picked up a PowerBar, his third of the day. As he got up on his scale, he ripped back the wrapper and took a hunk out of the thing.

202 pounds. Up from an all-time low in the hospital of 186.

Good. This was good.

He grabbed for his cane, not having to reach far for it. The shop's bathroom was about the size of a closet.

Stepping off the scale, he gently eased his full weight onto his left leg. The limb responded with a shot of pain and he backed off, looking down at it. The plaster cast had been replaced with a plastic one that had Velcro straps. Talk about improvements in quality of life. Even a half hour without the thing on was heaven.

He finished the PowerBar and tossed the wrapper.

A nine-pound gain in four weeks. Maybe his pants would stop hanging off his hips soon.

At six-four, he liked to weigh in at around 230. His big frame carried that kind of poundage well, all thick muscle, no fat. He figured it was going to take him three months to get back there if he gained two to three pounds a week. Which was doable. Every day, he was sucking back about five thousand calories. It was a lot to ask of the hot plate and dorm-size refrigerator he'd moved into the shop, but he was managing.

Man, he couldn't imagine Cassandra putting up with such a rudimentary kitchen. She'd want gourmet food for dinner. At a restaurant with a French chef and waiters in tuxedos—

Alex cursed. He really needed to put a lid on this compare-and-contrast thing he had going. Problem was, the closer her arrival date came, the more he looked at the way he lived from her perspective.

But the mental aerobics were useless. First of all, he wasn't going to be in the shop forever and second, it wasn't like she was moving in with him. She'd be staying at Gray's as she worked on White Caps.

So he needed to reel it in.

Hobbling out of the head, he crossed the shop with efficiency. The single room was not all that big and the floor wasn't cluttered. He was a neat guy to begin with, but considering how close he'd cut it with that leg of his, he wasn't taking a chance that he'd trip on something and take a nosedive.

He went over to the Nautilus cage he'd bought three weeks ago, its weight sets and benches gleaming silver and black. The piece of exercise equipment was by far the largest thing in the shop, about seven feet tall and four feet square with stations for isolating different muscle groups. One good thing about not having a life except for sailing was that what little money he'd accumulated had grown. Cutting a check for a professional-quality set up was no sacrifice.

He put on his earphones and clipped his MP3 player to the waistband of his nylon sweatpants. He worked out with no shirt because within minutes he was going to be covered with sweat and glad to have a bare chest. Sitting down on one of the benches, he eased onto his back and gripped a bar. When he pushed up, he felt his pectorals tighten as they accepted the weight.

With Nirvana blaring in his ears, he pumped through his exercises, tearing up his muscles so that they could rebuild stronger, better. The burn felt good. It felt healthy. It felt normal to him.

And he was hungry for normal.

He'd always made demands of his body and he expected it to respond with power. One of the hardest things about being laid up had been the weakness. Pain he could handle. Frailty was unbearable.

After his first set, he sat up, breathing hard and resting his arms on his knees. Usually Spike worked out with him, but today the guy was busy. Which was kind of a bummer. He liked having a buddy with him. Made the time pass quicker, plus Spike was pretty damn amusing.

Alex reached down and took a slug of water from a bottle.

The shop was really working out for him, he thought. Even if Cassandra would no doubt—

Stop it.

The twin bed he slept in was right next to the potbellied stove. December was really cold stuff this far north, and with his tendency for kicking off the covers when the nightmares came, he needed to be close to a heat source at night. His clothes were in duffel bags lying open and pushed against the wall, like drawers on the floor. Shoes were in an orderly line in front of them. Fleeces and jackets were hanging on pegs. Laundry went into a wicker basket.

Everything had its place.

All of the order made him think about Cassandra. Why? Who the hell knew. What didn't make him think of her?

Tilting his head around, he glanced out of the shop's

picture window at White Caps. His family's home looked as if it had been bombed and abandoned with all the plastic sheets covering burned-out windows and doors. It was hard to believe the place was ever going to be right again, but if anyone could fix it, Cassandra could.

When Frankie and Joy had campaigned to have her take on the project, they'd shown him photographs of her work. She'd designed and constructed houses, additions and out-buildings all over America and specialized in re-habbing antiques. She had an absolute genius for making the new look old.

So, professionally speaking, she was perfect for what they needed. There had been no way he could refuse.

Alex lay back down and gripped the bar again.

Plus he hadn't really wanted to refuse.

It had been so hard to see her leave Gray's those many weeks ago. Like a pathetic idiot, he'd watched from a window as she'd walked out of the house with O'Banyon. The man had had his hand at the small of her back while he'd guided her to his Mercedes and settled her in it.

The two of them going off together had made Alex grit his teeth so hard his gums had gone numb. He'd wanted to tear her out of that car and take her upstairs to the bed he slept in and keep her there by lying on her with his naked body.

But of course he'd let her go. And as those taillights had flared at the end of the driveway, it was clear she belonged in a fancy car with a man like O'Banyon. She was a refined kind of woman who was used to being on Manhattan's A-list. Living in a penthouse on Park Avenue. Wearing beautiful clothes.

Alex was a comparative savage and he always had been. Since day one, he'd had a deep core inside of him that was

uncivilized. And not as in cursing-in-mixed-company uncivilized, as in primitive-male uncivilized. The real world,
the modern world, didn't have a lot of places for a man like
him. He belonged where the beast inside of him could be
free to roam. He belonged on the ocean.

O'Banyon, on the other hand, would be fine and dandy
at one of Cassandra's parties. That lady-killer had plenty
of hard in him, that was obvious, but there was a high-gloss
sheen over all that rough and tough. When he escorted
Cassandra out on the town, no doubt he showed up in the
right suit and treated her like a queen and pressed palms
with the best of them.

Mr. Slick probably even knew how to waltz.

Alex let the bar go and sat up, grabbing a towel and
using it to wipe his face.

O'Banyon was definitely the type of man she should
be with, though it was a little surprising she'd moved on,
only a matter of months after Reese's death. But then
again, why should she be alone if she didn't want to be?
Mourning and a new lover didn't have to be mutually ex-
clusive. She could miss her husband and still not want to
spend the nights by herself.

O'Banyon was no doubt taking good care of her. Alex
might not like the guy, but there hadn't been a stupid bone
in that big body. The man had to know the rarity of what
he held in his hands.

Alex lay back down, grabbed the bar and pushed up
hard, feeling his pecs burn as though the muscles were
shredding apart.

Cassandra pulled up in front of White Caps and turned
off the Range Rover's engine. The Rover had been Reese's

birthday present to her the year before last. He'd maintained he felt safer with her in a big car, but she'd always thought it was more than she needed.

Now, she could see his point. Here in Saranac Lake there was a dusting of snow on the ground already. As winter pressed on and the drifts piled up, she was going to appreciate the traction and the mass of the Rover. Besides, all her luggage had fit in the back.

She looked at the house briefly, a clinical review that confirmed her first impressions and refreshed her memory. Then her eyes slid over to the large barn behind it. A tendril of white smoke drifted lazily from a chimney stack.

Alex was living there now. His sister had told her so.

And he was doing much better. His leg had been spared and he was healing up well.

Cass got out of the car. The cold air felt good, a brisk handshake of sorts that welcomed her to the Adirondacks.

She'd been tempted to go to Gray's right away so she could unpack and relax a little. She'd driven up from the city after a breakfast meeting this morning and was still in the Escada suit she'd put on at 6:00 a.m. But she wanted to review the original set of plans over dinner, and according to Frankie, the drawings were somewhere in the workshop.

Besides, she wanted to rip the Band-Aid off when it came to seeing Alex.

It was going to be hard and she was dying to get the first meeting behind her. With him in the shop and her working on the house, she was going to be running into him a lot over the next three months, and she might as well get used to it.

Walking over to the barn, she decided the out-building was a real charmer. Painted a deep red with bright white trim, it was cheery from the outside even though the roof was bowed and the walls listed a little. Then again, the imperfections were probably why the place appealed. Its good nature was amplified by its disabilities.

She straightened the collar of her silk shirt. Fussed with the gold chain belt around her waist. She didn't know why she bothered. The last thing Alex Moorehouse was going to care about was what she wore.

Knowing him, his priority would be hustling her off to anywhere he wasn't.

The door to the shop had no knocker or bell to ring so she rapped on it. When there was no answer, she tried again.

As she waited, the cold became not so welcoming. It seeped through the fine wool of her suit, the chill nipping at her shoulder blades.

She blew some warm air into her hands and gave the knocking another shot. Her knuckles stung as they hit the wood, and she rubbed them against her hip.

Nothing. Maybe he wasn't there.

Stamping her high heels, she was debating whether to go back to the car when she heard something inside. A metal clinking sound.

Cass took the toggle handle and lifted upward. The door opened easily.

"Hello?"

The noise, a rhythmic shifting of sorts, got louder.

She slipped through the door and closed it, wanting to preserve the heat. As she turned around, her legs stopped working.

Oh…good…Lord.

Alex was flat on his back, pushing a tremendous amount of weight up and down on a Nautilus machine. He was shirtless, wearing only a pair of loose nylon pants. Sweat gleamed on his bare chest.

She told herself to look away and couldn't. His muscles moved with a coordinated power that was intimidating and…well, erotic. Under his smooth skin, all that bunching and releasing reminded her of the incredible moment they'd shared.

The one only she knew had actually happened.

He released the weights, a metal clank cutting through the room. Then he sat up and focused ahead as if in a trance. He was breathing deeply, and a hissing noise came out of the earphones he had on.

She was about to clear her throat when his head snapped around.

His frown was totally expected.

"I knocked," she said. "A number of times."

With a jerk of his hand, his earphones popped out and dangled between his legs.

"I knocked," she repeated.

His eyes flicked over her, a quick head-to-toe review that was about as passionate as what she'd done to his family's house out in her car. He reached to his waist and unclipped a little black square.

Without saying a word, he picked a cane off the floor, stood up and limped away from her. His back was every bit as strong as the front of him was, the muscles fanning out from his spine. He had a black tattoo that covered his right shoulder blade: a beautiful, old-fashioned compass, like something you'd see on a medieval map.

What a difference a month made, she thought. His body was getting back into fighting shape and he seemed so much healthier.

When he bent down and grabbed a T-shirt out of a line of duffels on the floor, she didn't watch as he pulled it on.

"Your sister said the plans to White Caps are somewhere in here." She glanced around.

How did he fit on that twin bed? she wondered.

When she heard his footsteps, she brought her head up. He was coming over to her.

No, he was heading for the little refrigerator that was under a wooden table in the corner by the door.

God, she wished he'd say something.

He took out three small cans and lined them up in a row. One by one, he cracked them open.

She was about to start doing cartwheels to get his attention when he broke the silence.

"You're early. I thought you weren't coming until next week."

"I wanted to get started. Which is why I'm looking for the plans."

"I haven't seen any around here," he said, picking up the first can and downing it in one shot. He pitched the empty into the trash and went for number two. "But I'll help you look after I finish getting through these."

As if the consumption were a workout in and of itself.

"What's that you're drinking?" she asked.

"Ensure. Good source of vitamins and calories. Tastes like vanilla-flavored wallpaper paste."

"Um, you're looking much better." Actually, he was looking out-of-this-world good. His coloring was back. His strength, too, clearly.

But he had yet to meet her eyes, so she couldn't get a read on his emotions.

No, that wasn't true. His mood was easy to read. He was tolerating her.

When he'd polished off the third can, he nodded over his shoulder. "If the drawings are anywhere, they'll be in the back."

Alex went slowly over to a door. When he opened it, a cold draft shot into the room.

He flipped on a light switch. "I'll be right back."

"I want to help."

"Then wait here."

"Don't be silly."

"Fine, but you're going to end up on your ass in those shoes."

Cass went over and got a gander at the rest of the barn. Her eyes widened. "And you're going to be better-off with a cast in there?"

The place stretched out for some sixty feet and it was filled to capacity. Snowblowers and lawnmowers and an old truck and…was that an anti-tank gun? The barn aisle was a graveyard for half-dead machines and the menagerie was in total disorder. There wasn't even a pathway through the jungle of jagged edges.

She felt as if she needed a tetanus shot just to sniff the air.

With Alex in the lead, they picked their way over to a fireproof safe the size of a love seat. The cast-iron big boy was probably from the thirties or forties and made her think of old-fashioned bankers with visors sitting under little green-shaded lamps.

Alex twisted the dial a couple of times and then pushed down on the brass handle. She peered over his shoulder. The inside was crammed with documents that were catalogued with the same precision as the stuff in the barn's belly. Alex reached fearlessly into the mess and put it all into order while reviewing the papers.

Funny, for all his brute manliness, he was a tidy kind of guy. Back in the shop where he lived, all of his things were neat and in a place that made sense.

The legacy of years spent on boats, she thought.

"Not in there?" she asked as he shut the safe.

"No."

He got to his feet more quickly than she'd expected. As she jerked back, her heel caught on a tangle of thick rope, and gravity did its job, pulling her off balance. She grabbed the first thing that came into range.

Alex's arm.

As he absorbed her weight, he didn't shift his position in the slightest. His shoulders tightened and his biceps thickened, but other than that he was perfectly still.

This was the Alex she had always known. Powerful. Immovable.

His forearm was so hard. Warm. Strong.

"I warned you about those shoes," he said gruffly.

She let go and rubbed her hands on her skirt. "Shoes weren't the problem. Not having eyes in the back of my head was."

Unexpectedly, the corner of his mouth lifted.

"There's another place we can look." He nodded toward the door they'd come through. "You first. And don't worry, my eyes will be on your back."

As she turned, she sensed his height looming behind her. And felt him looking at her, watching her move.

Yeah, well, if he was staring, it was because he thought she was going to fall on her butt again.

When they returned to the shop, he went over to a roll-top desk and peeled back its cover. Dozens of drafting plans popped out, the blue paper lengths curled up and tied with little white strings.

"This looks like my desk at the office," she said, catching a few. "Who was the architect in your family?"

"They're boat construction documents." He gathered up some and put them aside.

She unrolled one of them. The skeleton of a yacht was rendered with architectural precision, all the measurements and angles noted with a careful hand.

"This is beautiful. Who—"

"My father." Alex pulled open a drawer and took out a key, then limped over to a closet. He slid out a three-by-five-foot lockbox. After he lifted the lid, he said, "Here they are."

He handed her a leather document roll.

She started to open it.

"I'm sure they're in there."

Read: You can look at them somewhere else, she thought.

Cass took the hint and went for the door.

"If you're staying through the weekend," he said, "you should know there's a storm coming. Going to be hard to get out on Sunday."

She glanced over her shoulder. "I'm not leaving on Sunday."

"Good."

"I'll be here up until the holidays."

He frowned. "For the whole month? Doing what?"

"The job you and your sisters hired me for."

Alex's eyes went over her body. He lingered for a split second on the gold chain at her waist.

"Is there a problem?" she said.

"Don't get me wrong here. One of my best crew

members is a woman and she's tougher than most of my men. But it's hard to imagine you with a hammer."

Wait until you get a load of me tomorrow morning, she thought, reaching for the door.

She paused. "The subcontractors I've hired show up early. I'll tell them to be quiet so they won't disturb you."

"Don't bother. I'm an early riser." His eyes narrowed, as if a thought had just occurred to him. "Gray and Joy are gone, right? They're back in Manhattan."

"Yes, they said we'd have the house to ourselves."

"We?"

She nodded, glad that Libby, the housekeeper, and Ernest, the golden retriever, were going to be at the mansion with her. When she'd talked to the other woman on the phone, Libby had cheerfully agreed to split the KP duties. With Ernest on cleanup.

As Alex's face darkened, Cass turned away, thinking it was definitely time to go.

But at least she'd gotten through their first meeting in one piece.

"See you tomorrow," she murmured while going out the door.

Alex watched the Range Rover disappear down the drive.

He had not been prepared, he thought.

He had not been prepared to look up and see her standing before him. Had not been prepared to have her eyes on his naked chest. Had not been prepared for his body's reaction.

He'd...oh, man, he'd hardened for her. It had happened in a split second. Her eyes on his skin, and suddenly all he could feel was that dream.

Alex rubbed his eyes, trying not to picture O'Banyon and Cassandra in that big house alone. With all those beds. Surely Mr. Slick had things to keep him in the city, though. If he was some kind of big-deal investment banker, he had to be going back. Soon.

Oh, this was going to be such fun.

Alex went over to his father's desk and stared at the rolled tubes of sailboat renderings. He picked up the one Cassandra had unraveled and flattened it out.

The lines were beautifully drawn and the design was good, stability and speed assured by the shape of the hull.

Alex frowned. The stern was wrong. The stern needed to be narrower.

He sank down into the chair. Studied the plans more closely. Used them as a way to get his mind off Cassandra.

Before he knew it, he'd grabbed a pencil and was very lightly sketching in a change here and there. The Mead #2 felt good in his hand. And the buzz in his head, the concentration, the parallel processing as his analytical skills met his instincts for wind and current, made him feel...

He put the pencil down. Rolled the drawing up tightly. Put the thing back and closed the desk up tight.

Resting his hand on the wood, he thought about his father.

The two of them had had little in common.

Ted had been an easygoing man. Uncomplicated. Content. He'd loved his wife and three children and been satisfied living on the lakeshore and running the B&B. He'd enjoyed refurbishing boats and dabbling with yacht designs but not enough to really break into the business. Still, he'd been happy. Period.

Alex had been born with a fire in his belly. His mother had said his terrible twos lasted until he was twelve and then he'd embraced teenage rebellion as if it were a religion. He'd missed curfews, skipped school, slacked off in his classes. He'd been a varsity letterman in football and basketball, his only successes, and he'd tolerated the practices and the theatrics of the coaches because it was the only way he could compete.

Then he'd found sailing.

Saranac Lake had a very rich summer community, and competitive yachting was a very rich kind of sport. He'd been introduced to it through the guys he snuck long-necks and coffin nails with in July and August, and soon enough, he was crewing on their families' boats off Newport, Rhode Island.

His reputation as a hotheaded, never-say-die, ocean-faring psycho didn't take long to get established. He'd started by winning singles races and then graduated to the bigger boats because, even though he was young, he was good with teams of men. He dominated them, controlled them, motivated them. Made them win.

Before he knew it, he'd blown off a football scholarship to Duke and taken to yachting all year round. Family holidays, birthdays, anniversaries, they'd all been lost to his relentless schedule. Without him even realizing it, a couple of years passed before he returned to Saranac. Even then he came home only because his parents had been killed in an accident on the lake.

Thinking back to the decade before the tragedy, he could hardly recognize his younger self. Which made sense because after his parents died, Alex had turned into someone else.

In the wake of losing them, he'd had no frame of reference for his grief and guilt, so he shut down. He could remember exactly where he'd stood when the change had come over him.

He'd needed a suit for the funeral, because it was the respectful thing to wear. He'd gone to his father's closet and gently rifled through the clothes as if they were made of tissue paper. There had been so many things he'd never seen the man wear, so many seasons lost. He had wanted to cry, had been on the verge of it, but then Frankie had come into the room. When he'd told her what he was looking for, she'd said that the only suit their father owned was the one he was getting buried in.

As Alex had turned to leave, he'd seen a hanger on the bed. It had been one of those wooden ones with an arm you could slip the slacks through and clip into place. He'd been staring at it when Frankie picked the thing up and carried it back to the closet, inserting it between a flannel shirt and a sweater that was sagging out of shape at the shoulders.

"I suppose I'll have to…empty this all out," she'd said in a dull voice.

At that moment something had clicked off in him. Or maybe just…got up and left.

He'd worn khakis and a black sweater to the service. And he'd left a half hour after his parents had been put into the ground.

It was the pinnacle of his selfishness. The absolute zenith of his egocentric nature. To cut and run at that moment was not only cowardly, but cruel. He'd suspected it then. He knew it for a fact now.

Thereafter, Frankie had raised Joy and kept White Caps alive. She'd also lost a fiancé in the process. Lost her life, in a way.

Alex had gone back to racing, but he was different at the helm. What had once been reckless passion got turned into an icy, focused control that left him utterly unflappable. In the shutting off, the cooling down, he was transformed from a good sailor into one of the greats.

So many America's Cup trophies had been brought home because of his leadership. So many laudations, so much awe, until he was worshiped as The Warrior. Meanwhile, Frankie and Joy had been here. Fending for themselves, unsupported by him. They must have assumed he'd forgotten about them, but he never had. He'd thought of them always.

Just done jack about it.

Even now, with him here at home, his sisters haunted him. They were ghosts just as Cassandra was, born out of his failings as a brother, a friend. A man.

Alex took his hand off the desk.

There was a time when he had disdained his father for wanting to live such a simple life. Now, he was fairly certain that when Ted died, he'd shaken St. Peter's hand with few regrets.

For a man to have been a good father and husband, to have taken care of his own, to have loved his community and had the quiet respect of neighbors and friends, that was a life led well, led with honor.

Far better than what Alex had to show for himself.

All those trophies and plaques he'd won were in a storage unit in Newport.

Unlike his father, the culmination of his life's accomplishments was nothing more than a ragged landing pad for dust.

Chapter Six

The following day Cassandra met the crew she'd hired at the site and took them through the house. She'd culled the men's names from Frankie who had used each one in some capacity or another over the years. They were middle-aged, strong and grateful for the winter work because by definition construction was seasonal this far north. After November, with all the snowstorms and cold temperatures, it was difficult to do much outdoors beyond ice fishing or hurrying home.

Plus, White Caps was a cush job. With the windows and the doorways sealed with plastic, and a propane heater blaring like a jet engine, the place was warm and out of the wind. The only possible determent was having a woman for a boss, but none of them seemed to have a problem with that. At least not on their first morning together.

If any of them did develop an attitude, she'd handle the problem the way she always did. She knew houses from their concrete basement slabs to their roofing nails and all the wall studs and floorboards in between. After having discussed the project thoroughly with Frankie, studied the plans until midnight last evening and been at White Caps since six this morning, she also knew this particular building. She understood exactly what had to be done and in what order.

So there was no question that she couldn't answer. No problem that she couldn't reason out logically. No obstacle to progress that she couldn't surmount. That knowledge, coupled with how hard she was going to work, would cure any testosterone-laden God complex that might crop up.

And lunch brought in with some frequency wouldn't hurt morale, either.

She glanced down at her clothes, thinking of Alex's comment the day before. The blue jeans, fleece and parka she was wearing were from Freeport, Maine, not Madison Avenue. Dressed in all this L.L. Bean, she wondered whether he could see her with a hammer now.

Cass looked at the men and gestured around the decimated kitchen.

"We're starting here. The counters and cabinets need to be stripped out. Appliances, too. Sheetrock goes. Do not remove any of the joists in the ceiling, even though they're burned out. I need to do a structure eval on the second story before I decide whether we'll replace all of them or some of them." She pointed to the floor. "The hardwood is strong enough to support you, but it's all got to go. We'll wait until the space is clean before we take it up. Dumpster is arriving at ten."

Tim, a squat, dark-haired guy with an easy smile, nodded. "You want the electrics capped?"

She nodded. "Fuse box is shut down in the cellar. Gas and water are off, as well. At nine, a generator's coming so we can run the power tools and lights. Lunch is on me today and it's coming at eleven-thirty."

"What are we eating?" he asked.

"Subs."

"Nice."

She returned his smile and looked at the other three. Lee, Greg and Bobbie were nodding with approval.

"Any questions?"

"Do the subs come with chips?" Lee said with mock gravity.

She smirked. "Yes. Frito's or Ruffles, your choice. How about any questions on the house?"

They shook their heads.

"Let's get to work. I'll be upstairs checking the floor stability."

Alex fished around the duffel bag, holding a towel at his waist.

No boxers.

He eyed his laundry pile. He didn't mind going bareback in his jeans and he'd work out buck naked if he had to, provided Spike wore a blindfold. But socks were an issue. His feet were always cold, and there was no way he could sleep in dirty socks.

It looked as if he would have to go to Gray's.

And if he happened to run into O'Banyon and had to tread on the guy's toes a little? Well, that would just be a flaming pity, wouldn't it?

He glanced out the picture window. The Range Rover was parked in front of White Caps. Alongside it were two pickups and an old Trans Am.

He'd been asleep when Cassandra had arrived, and considering he'd woken up at six-thirty, he had to wonder when she'd come. He'd also missed seeing the men because he'd been in the shower.

So it was time to head over and check out the crew.

Alex drew on his jeans, pulled on his last pair of clean socks and re-secured the cast over his pant leg. He shrugged on a T-shirt and a fleece, popped his free foot into a boot and headed for the door with his cane.

Outside, the ground was frozen solid, the light snow like powdered sugar over the lawn. His breath came out in puffs of white, and the cold hit his cheeks like a slap.

He paused, measuring the sky. It was a dull, gunmetal gray. Snow was definitely coming tonight.

From the direction of White Caps, a wrenching sound cut through the still air and then something was tossed out what had been the kitchen alcove's window. The tangle of metal bounced on the lawn. Part of the stainless steel cabinets, he surmised.

Alex went over to the house. As he walked through the back door's plastic sheet, he took stock of the men. Four guys, all mid- to late-thirties. He was bigger than all of them, and the deference in their eyes told him they'd noticed that, too.

"Where is she?" he demanded.

"Who are you?" replied a squat guy wearing red flannel.

Alex liked the guy's suspicion. "I'm a Moorehouse."

"Oh…wow. You're Frankie's older brother. The sailor. Who was missing—"

"Yeah. Where's Cassandra?"

"She's upstairs." The man pointed with his hammer.

Alex eyed the scorched ceiling and hated the thought of her standing on any of the floorboards up there.

"Thanks."

As he used the front stairs, he could hear the men's hushed voices. Words like "storm," "dead" and "injured" made him hurry to get out of earshot.

When he got to the top landing, he went over and pushed open the fire doors that separated the staff quarters from where the guests stayed. Walking down a plain, unadorned hallway, he looked in each one of the rooms, not lingering. They reminded him of his sisters, his parents, himself, and he found the burned-out floors and blackened walls depressing.

Down at the end of the corridor he heard a squeak, as if a board were being pulled up.

Must be another of the crew, he thought.

He peered into one of the bathrooms, expecting to see Cassandra standing in the middle of the chaos wearing some kind of perfect outfit. And high heels.

Where was she?

He headed for the noise, opening the door to the last of the baths, the one that was directly over the damage in the kitchen. There was a guy on the floor dressed in a hooded fleece, navy parka and blue jeans. He had a crowbar wedged under a plank of hardwood and was tearing it up. A pile of boards was next to him.

"Do you know where Cassandra is?"

The guy looked over his shoulder. "Hi, Alex."

As he frowned, Cassandra pulled off the hood. Her hair

was tied back in a ponytail. She had no makeup on. And her cheeks were blazing from exertion.

Alex blinked a couple of times.

Then ran his eyes over the baggy pants that had faded paint splotches on them. The heavy outerwear. The scuffed work boots.

If she was lovely in couture, she was crazy attractive in work clothes. He had a sudden urge to shut the door behind him and get under all that fleece.

She smiled a little. "Do you want a tour of what I plan to do?"

Actually, he'd only come to stare the men in the face so they'd know if they made trouble for her, they were going to answer to him. With that mission having been accomplished down in the kitchen, he really hadn't had a reason to go looking for her at all. Other than to see her.

But then he remembered.

"I'm going to Gray's late this afternoon," he said. "Just wanted you to know. I do my laundry there."

"Okay. Do you want to stay for dinner?"

Uh-huh, right. As if he needed to watch O'Banyon drool all over her.

Then again, ruining the guy's night by stealing a romantic dinner right out from under his nose had some appeal.

"Yeah, I think I will. I'll be over around six."

As darkness fell, Cassandra walked into Gray's kitchen, grateful for the warmth and the fact that the place didn't smell like propane.

"Libby?" she called out while peeling off layers. "I'm home."

There was a patter of dog feet, and Ernest came down the back stairs, moving slower than usual.

"Hey, big guy." She crouched down. "You look a little droopy."

The retriever circled in front of her, offering a lack-luster wag before he lay down and rolled over onto his back. She stroked his belly as Libby came in from the stairs.

"Hi, there!" The woman pulled on her wool coat and wrapped a scarf around her neck. "How was your first day on the job?"

"It went just fine." Cass tried to keep her voice level. "Are you going somewhere for dinner?"

"My brother called. His wife fell down today and the two of them are in pretty rough shape. Her, for obvious reasons. Him, because he doesn't know how to heat up a can of soup without needing a fire extinguisher. I figure, if I don't get dinner made for them, you'll have another charred mess of a house to work on. But don't worry, I cooked an oven-stuffer roaster and left it in the refrigerator for you. I whipped up a salad, also."

"Thank you. That was very thoughtful."

Oh, God. Dinner. With Alex. Alone.

"Say, are you okay, Cass?"

She stood up. "I'm fine. Just need a quick shower. Has Ernest been fed?"

"In a manner of speaking. He tore into a package of cookies that had slipped out of a grocery bag. Spent most of the afternoon in the yard." Libby came over and rubbed the dog's head. "No more Fig Newtons for you, right?"

Ernest heaved a big sigh as if answering.

"I'll give him a little extra love," Cass murmured.

"He'd appreciate that." Libby headed for the door. "Oh, and don't wait up for me. My brother's a long talker."

Twenty minutes later Cass put the blow-dryer down and didn't bother to brush her hair out. There was no need to worry about the stuff. No need to put makeup on, either. It was the country, for one thing, and no matter where she was, she had no reason to primp for Alex, either.

Talk about surprised, she thought. She'd never expected him to take her up on the dinner invite. She'd only put it out there to be polite.

Cass threw on what she thought of as her dorm clothes: leggings and a floppy white turtleneck. Then she put thick cotton socks to good use and stuffed her feet into a pair of moccasin slippers. When she got to the kitchen, she went over to the refrigerator and figured she might as well wrestle up dinner. No doubt Alex was going to eat fast and run.

"Have a good shower?" he asked from behind her.

She wheeled around. "Holy…!"

"Sorry. Didn't mean to sneak up on you." His eyes were hooded as they drifted over her hair.

"No, it's fine. I, uh…" It was not fine. She was *not* fine. Especially as she looked him over.

Alex had on a pair of jeans that hung low on his hips and a black turtleneck sweater. His dark hair was brushed back and seemed a little damp. As he stood under the recessed lighting, he was so handsome, it was hard to take in his presence without blinking a lot. Worse, she had to force herself to forget she had a clear picture of his bare chest. And knew exactly what the skin across his stomach felt like.

"Ah, Libby left us something," she said, turning to the

refrigerator and thinking maybe she should get in it. The kitchen suddenly felt two degrees away from tropical.

She thought of his hand leading hers down his torso and on to his…

Make that volcanic.

"Are we going to eat in here?" he drawled.

She put the chicken on the counter and went back for the salad. "Absolutely. No reason to be formal."

When she pivoted around, Alex was eyeing the swinging door as if waiting for someone to come through it. Someone he wasn't particularly fond of, going by his razor eyes.

"So, you looked surprised to see me this morning," she said as she grabbed a plate and started cutting into the roast.

"Do you need some help?"

"Were you surprised?" It was perverse, but she wanted to hear him say it. She wanted the satisfaction of knowing she'd thrown him, even if it was just a little.

There was a pause. "Yeah. I was."

She put the plate of chicken in the microwave and sent it on a merry-go-round ride. Then she took the salad over to the table, grabbed a bottle of white wine from the refrigerator and tried to remember where the napkins were.

Somewhere over to the left. About where Alex was standing with his cane resting on his thigh and his cast kicked out in front of him.

"Would you get the napkins? They're behind you. I think."

His eyes flipped to the door again and he smiled darkly. "My pleasure."

"Why do you keep looking over there?"

But he was bent down, opening drawers, and obviously didn't hear her.

Maybe it was the dog. Ernest could be a lot to handle,

and for a man with a cast, an eighty-pound canine flying across a room was a dangerous thing.

"You don't need to worry about him," she said. "He's staying upstairs."

Alex looked over his shoulder. "Oh, really."

"He wasn't feeling well."

"Poor baby," he murmured. "So it's just you and me for dinner?"

She nodded. "Don't feel bad. I gave him a lot of attention before you came."

Alex frowned, a dark emotion settling into his eyes.

"I'm sure you did," he said with an edge.

As Alex grabbed two napkins, he tried not to imagine the kind of "extra attention" she'd given O'Banyon.

"You don't think you love him or something, do you?" he blurted out.

Oh, *shut up,* Moorehouse.

Cass frowned and then laughed a little. "I adore him. Although he can be a lot to handle…you know, always all over me."

Terrific. Like he needed to know O'Banyon was a hungry lover. With stamina.

God, maybe he should just leave. Before he found out how big the man's—

"Would you like some wine?" she asked.

No, actually, he'd like a concussion. At least that way he'd stop talking. And thinking.

And looking.

Cass was sexy as hell tonight. Black leggings and a loose turtleneck that hung past her hips. Her red hair was down and curlier than he'd ever seen it, as if she'd let it dry naturally or hadn't brushed it out. He wanted to sink his hands into the thick waves and angle her head back and kiss her until they both went weak.

"Alex?"

"Yeah?"

"Wine?"

"Sure. I'll get the glasses. And the silver."

The microwave dinged. She took the plate out with a potholder and carried it over to the table while he got the knives and forks.

Before they sat down, he went and put his wash in the dryer, peeling the nylon sweats away so they could air dry.

When he came back in, she was at the table, pouring the chardonnay. She looked tired.

"What time did you get to the house this morning?" he asked as he sat down. They traded bowls and plates until they'd served themselves.

"I don't remember."

"I woke up early. You were already there."

"Don't worry, you're not paying me by the hour," she chided gently, pushing her food around.

He finished what was on his plate. Went back for seconds. Was halfway through them when he realized she'd barely taken a bite. He lowered his fork.

"What's wrong?" he asked, nodding to her food.

She shrugged. "Nothing."

"Why aren't you eating?"

Cassandra shook her head and went back to shifting lettuce leaves around.

Then she murmured, "You know, I'm thinking of selling Reese's penthouse."

"The one in Manhattan?"

When she nodded, he thought that was a weird way of referring to the place, considering it was her home, too.

"Where will you go?"

"I want something smaller. It's not that I need the money. I just…" She took a sip from her wineglass and pushed her plate away. "Do you ever…get lonely?"

He stiffened and said the only thing that occurred to him. "I want you to eat more."

She had another small drink. "Yeah, that's probably a silly question, isn't it? You aren't the type who needs other people."

Alex jabbed at her plate with his fork. "You worked hard today. You need to eat."

If they kept this up, he thought, they would probably finish the conversations by themselves. Maybe move on to two new ones.

There was a noise from upstairs.

"Excuse me, I better go check on him." Cass got up and went to the back stairwell.

Alex frowned, wondering why she and O'Banyon weren't staying in the guest rooms in the front of the house.

"Oh, there you are," she said, leaning up against the banister. "You okay, Ernest?"

Ernest?

She patted her thighs. "You want to go out?"

There was a soft padding noise and the jingle of a collar, then the golden retriever came into the kitchen looking sleepy. He wagged at Alex, but went straight for the back door as Cass held it open.

"Cassandra."

"Hmm?" She shut the thing and came back to the table.

"Who else is in this house right now?"

She tilted her head to the side. "No one. Libby went to her brother's. Why?"

Alex wiped his mouth with his napkin and eased back in the chair.

Idiot.

Jealous idiot.

Although mistaking O'Banyon for a dog did make some sense.

As she looked at him, he took a deep breath. "Tell you what. If you eat, I'll try to…talk."

Her luminous green stare became rapt. "So you do get lonely?"

"Pick up that fork."

When she started eating, he took a drink and cleared his throat.

"No, I don't get lonely." He paused. "I, ah…I don't get along with people that well."

Her eyes widened as if she were surprised that he'd elaborated.

Well, that made two of them.

"You don't get along…?" she prompted softly.

He shook his head. "Never really have. I mean, I'm great with them in a competitive environment. Otherwise, they make me…nervous." When she stared at him, nearly openmouthed, he bristled. "What?"

"Sorry. It's hard to imagine you scared of anything. Or anybody."

"I did *not* say scared."

Was that a smirk? He couldn't tell because she'd covered her lips with her wineglass.

"So why do they make you anxious?" she asked.

"How about some more stuffing?"

"I don't—"

"Yeah, I don't feel like saying much more, either."

She dug that serving spoon so far into the chicken, he could have sworn it came out the other side.

God, he hoped she got full quickly.

As Cass lifted her fork, she cocked her eyebrow. She had to keep Alex talking. Learning something, anything, about the man was unexpected. To have him admit to a weakness of sorts was extraordinary.

He took a long drink from his wineglass. "I never know what to say. In social situations. I mean, all that small talk? My mind just shuts down. That's one of the things I love about being on the ocean. No chatting. Plus every time I'm on land, people look at me like I'm some kind of god and it's just too weird."

His hand came up and pulled at the collar of his turtleneck.

Good Lord. Alex Moorehouse was shy.

It was like finding out the earth wasn't round. She had to recalibrate everything she knew.

He was still hard as nails, radiating a kind of male power that was inherently sensual and somewhat dangerous. But the idea that he had a vulnerability made him appealing as well as sexy.

When he shifted in his seat, she realized she was staring. Seriously staring.

She looked down at her plate.

"Reese and I got along," he murmured, "because he understood how I am. He liked all the attention. I couldn't stand the reporters, the fans. The parties. We worked. Together...we worked."

Cass felt an odd stirring in her chest. *The parties.*

She'd been well aware of how much Reese had liked the parties.

That was how she'd first learned for sure that he was cheating. He'd called her from one in Sydney, Australia. She'd heard the chatting and the music in the background and he'd reassured her it was just another celebration after a successful race. Right after they'd said goodbye and hung up, her phone had rung again. She'd answered it, and before she got to *hello,* she'd heard him whisper huskily, *Meet me upstairs in ten minutes. You know my room.* Then the phone had gone dead.

He'd never realized he'd hit Redial instead of whatever number he'd programmed into his cell.

Right after the incident, she'd thought about confronting him, and had agonized over it. But in the end she'd let it go. The status quo had somehow seemed more important than her anger.

Tonight, though, she wished she had put it all out in the open. Preserving the peace and the stability of her life had seemed so important back then. Except now, after the months of chaos following his death, she wondered why she'd protected the lie. An illusion of calm was in fact no peace at all.

The sound of wine clucking into a glass brought her back to the present. Alex put the bottle down and stared at what he had poured.

"You must miss him," she said.

Alex rubbed his eyes. "Yeah. I do. He was my partner and my friend."

"I thought you would come to the funeral. When you didn't, that's how I knew you were really injured."

"I just couldn't be there. I heard it was a beautiful service."

"It was. He would have liked it. All the people. The speeches. He was loved by so many. I can't tell you the number of letters I got from all over the world. He seemed to have friends everywhere."

There was a long silence. Then Alex asked, "How are you getting along without him?"

Cass pushed a piece of chicken around her plate. "Okay. The adjustment is slow."

Alex looked at her strangely.

"Is that the wrong answer?" she murmured.

"No." His navy blue eyes narrowed and he considered her with the full force of his intellect. Which made her feel like she was under a spotlight. "I guess I just expected something different."

"The my-life-is-over response?" she said sadly.

"Yeah. Maybe."

Cass put her fork down and moved her plate away. "Reese meant a lot to me. So of course I miss him."

But her life was not over, and somehow that felt like a betrayal, almost equal to his with the other women.

"You know," Alex said, "he used to talk about you all the time. On the boats. When the work was done and the crew was sacking out, he would sit in the cockpit with me and talk about you."

"Really?"

"Why are you surprised?"

Because if he'd really loved me, he wouldn't have needed the other women, she thought.

God, why was she just figuring this out now, when he was gone?

Then again maybe it did make some sense. Reese had been like a Klieg light, brilliant, distracting, gathering fanfare around him. Between keeping up with him and working, she'd had little time for reflection. And maybe she'd liked that.

"He used to talk about you, too," Cass said. "He used to tell me about all the things you did, how you handled things. He respected no one more than he did you, Alex. He used to say you were the brother he never had, the son he didn't get and the father he lost too soon."

She glanced up. Alex seemed to have retreated into himself, tension suffusing his face, darkening it.

"I am none of those things," he muttered.

"To him you were. And I have to say, I always felt badly for his son, Daniel, because of it."

"How old is D.C. now?"

"He's almost thirty. He's inherited the businesses and I think he's going to do very well. Sean's going out of his way to help him. The three of us had dinner before I came here and it was clear how much D.C. is capable of absorbing. He's very smart."

Alex drained his wineglass and nodded at her plate. "Looks like you're finished."

"What—oh, with the food. Yes, I think I am."

Alex pushed back his chair and got to his feet. When he started to clean up, she said, "I'll get all this. Don't worry about it."

He nodded and flipped open his cell phone. A moment later he said, "Hey, man. Got time for a pickup? Yeah? Thanks."

While she let the dog in and cleared the table, Alex disappeared into the laundry room. Ten minutes later, he came out with a duffel bag. His timing was perfect. A pair of headlights swung around the drive.

"When's Libby getting home?" he asked.

"Later. She said her brother likes to talk."

"You going to be okay here all by yourself?"

"Yes. Yes, thank you."

He lingered for a moment by the door. "Good night, then."

Alex waved Spike off and let himself into the shop. The fire had burned down in the potbellied stove, so it was cold. He restoked the embers and sat on the bed, but a minute later he was outside, carefully walking over the lawn to the lake. The snowstorm had arrived, thick flakes falling in the cold night air. The chilly wind blowing off the water whittled away his clothing and seeped into his skin, going deep into his bones.

Reese meant a lot to me. So of course I miss him.

Alex stepped out onto the dock, moving cautiously so he didn't slip.

Her words had not been those of a heartbroken woman, he thought. And her tone had been flat. Factual.

Somehow he'd assumed she'd be a wreck.

He looked down at the churning water, a cold spray hitting his legs as waves jumped at the dock and splintered.

He told himself he should be impressed that Cassandra was moving on. New lover. New project. Soon, a new home. He was sure Reese would have approved of her making a fresh start.

But that was yet another reason why his friend had deserved her and he didn't. If Alex had been her husband, he would have wanted her to mourn him every day for the rest of her life. He would want her to be as ruined as he'd be if he lost her.

And didn't that make him a real prince.

He stared at the lake until his body grew so cold his large muscle groups started twitching to generate heat. He went back to the shop and shook the snow out of his hair. Then he stripped naked and put on a fresh pair of socks. When he was settled on the bed, he shut his eyes.

Images of Cassandra came to him in the darkness. He pictured her eyes, green as fresh June leaves on a maple tree. He saw her tongue coming out for a little lick after she'd finished drinking. He recalled those black leggings stretched over her thighs and hips as she bent down to pet Ernest.

Alex's body came alive, lust chasing away the lingering chill. He grew heavy and hard between his legs, aching for her.

He rolled over and punched his pillow. The sheets shifting against his arousal made his jaw clench, and when he arched his back to try and release some tension, the heat rose even further. He pictured her lying beneath his naked body, her red hair in a wild tumble over his pillow, her skin so soft against his. He imagined being joined with her, going deep and sliding free only to plunge in again. He felt her grabbing on to his back as he drove his hips, heard his name on her lips as she climaxed.

Afterward, he saw himself holding her and watching her fall asleep.

Alex cursed in the darkness. The bastard in him just refused to let go of her. Even with all his guilt, even with the horrible knowledge of what he'd done, he couldn't control the visions or the hunger.

But he could make himself pay.

Lying in the dark, he opened himself up to the pain of

wanting what he couldn't have, knowing he deserved every last bit of what ailed him.

On the twin bed that was too small to hold him, he suffered and was glad for it.

Chapter Seven

A week later Cassandra parked the Rover at White Caps, grabbed her clipboard and headed for the house. As she passed by the Dumpster, she noted it was time for a pickup. Especially as they were going to tackle the Sheetrock removal in the dining room next.

Just before she went into the house, she looked up at the shop.

A big shape moved out of the picture window.

Alex had been watching her. Again.

He seemed to do that each time she came and went, and he always ducked away when she glanced toward the barn.

After their dinner together, she really wanted to reach out to him, she just wasn't sure how. Though if she was honest, she didn't only want to have him talk more about his grief. She wanted to learn other things about him. The glimpse she'd had of the man underneath the legend had been captivating.

So was the idea that he was warming up to her a little.

As Tim's truck came down the drive, she waved.

"Mornin', boss," he said as he got out. Lee and Greg were right behind him in the Trans Am. Then Bobbie pulled up in his truck.

The morning flew by, and when three-o'clock quitting time got close, Cassandra was exhausted from ripping out all the bathroom mirrors and vanities upstairs. She headed down to the kitchen and found the men clustered around a stubborn cabinet section they'd been trying to get free for the past week. They referred to the thing as Chunk, and when they weren't cursing at it, they were paying respect to its death grip on the house.

Chunk notwithstanding, the crew had done great work, and if they kept up this pace, she could have the plumber and the electrician start ahead of schedule. Re-piping and re-wiring White Caps was going to take some time, and with Christmas and New Year's coming up, they were going to lose a good ten days.

During the holidays everyone was taking a hiatus from the project. She was going back to Manhattan; the men were going to enjoy time off with their families. She told herself it would be good to get away because she'd been working long hours and not sleeping all that well. But she wasn't in a big hurry to leave the lake.

Her first Christmas without Reese, she thought. Her first birthday without him, too.

He'd loved surprising her with extravagant birthday presents on New Year's Eve, always trying to top himself. The culmination had been the year before. For her thirtieth, he'd rented the Metropolitan Museum of Art for the night and they'd strolled around the galleries arm in arm until they'd ended up in front of a table set for two. She'd been thrilled, thinking they'd spend a quiet evening together in front of her favorite Rembrandt, but then people had burst out into the room, friends and business associates of Reese's, all wishing her a happy birthday.

She'd told him that she'd loved it, of course. Because that was what he'd wanted to hear.

God, she'd kept so much from him, hadn't she?

"Ah, boss?"

"Sorry, Tim. What was that?"

"We gotta real problem with Chunk." He pointed to the corner. "The back's bolted into the wall, and we can't open it to get in with wrenches, because the firemen jumped all over the thing. We tried taking the doors off, but the hinges are all bent and the crowbar's not getting us anywhere."

Cass looked the cabinet over. It was directly across from the blown-out window in the alcove.

"Tim, how good's the traction on your truck?"

"The best. She's sporting a V8 under the hood and I got the chains on."

"Good. Back your beast around. I saw some rope in the barn. We're going to liberate Chunk." She jogged outside and bypassed the shop, using a door that went directly into the barn. Weeding through the machines, she found the thick, coiled length she'd tripped over that first day and dragged the dead weight through the snow back to the house.

Ten minutes later they had the rope wrapped around the belly of the cabinet.

"Run this out to your truck, Tim. When I give you the signal, I want just a little gas. Keep it light or we'll shred the wall. All we need is to strip the screws so the thing's detached, okay? We don't want to pull it out onto the lawn."

Tim smiled. "I got a soft foot. Don't you worry."

"Wait for my signal." She looked over at Lee, Greg and Bobbie, who were taking bets on whether Chunk or the Ford F-150 was going to win. "Stay back, boys."

She whistled and got out of the way. The rope tightened, strained and the cabinet was gently ripped from the wall. She waited until it was far enough out and whistled again. The rope went slack.

"Perfect." She reached down to untie the cabinet as the men high-fived each other.

She glanced up and smiled, only to see Alex standing in the kitchen's doorway. Furious.

"Tell your men to leave," he said. "Now."

The crew fell quiet as she got to her feet. "I beg your pardon?"

"You heard me. Or we're going to do this in front of them."

Cass frowned, but before her mouth could jump ahead of her brain, she checked her watch. It was quitting time, anyway.

"Okay." She nodded at Tim. "Great work with your truck. Thanks. Listen, let's just leave this until tomorrow."

The guys glanced at Alex. Looked back at her.

"You sure about that, boss?" Tim said, staring right in her eyes.

"Yes. I'll see you in the morning."

As car doors were shut and engines started, she and Alex stayed quiet, the tension flowing between them like the blue arc of a welder.

When the guys had pulled out, she said, "You want to tell me what that was all about?"

"What the *hell* are you thinking?"

As if the source of his ire was so flipping obvious? "I'm not a mind reader, Alex. You're going to have to be more specific."

He jabbed his finger to the floor. "Using this rope."

You've got to be kidding me, she thought. He gets territorial over a thirty-foot coil of nasty, dirty rope? Sure, she might have asked him, but the damn thing was no worse for wear.

She rolled her eyes and stepped past him. "You can have it back. We're finished."

As she bent down and started gathering the thing up, he grabbed her arm and snapped her body to his. Her ponytail swung around and landed between them.

"Did you think what would have happened if it broke?"

Cass pulled against his hold. Got absolutely nowhere. "It was strong enough."

"Luck, not planning."

"Will you let go—"

"I saw a man lose an eye when a rope just that size snapped on a mooring. Caught him right in the face. He thought the damn thing was strong enough, too."

"I was standing—"

"Not far enough away." He jerked her even closer. "Now, listen up. You're the contractor, not one of the workmen. I want you to cut it out with the hands-on stuff."

Cass took a deep breath before she told him to shove it. "Look, Alex—"

"You're not picking up another hammer. Or a crowbar. Or so much as a nail. Do we understand each other?"

Not in the slightest, she thought. No way was she going to stand for this heavy-handed, macho steak-head power trip of his.

She rose up on her tiptoes so she could get in tighter with his eyes. It was like using a step ladder to get level with a rooftop, but at least she made it to his jawline.

Her tone was hard. "You want me on this job? Fine. Dandy. Good. Then I'm in charge here, not you. You got a problem with the way I handle things? Fire me and get someone else."

He leaned down, his face so close to hers they were almost kissing. "Do you really want me to can you? Because I will. In a heartbeat."

They glared at each other, the air crackling.

He lifted her hand by the wrist. Twisting it around, he inspected the black-and-blue mark on the back. "How'd you get this?"

"None of your business."

"How many others are there? And where?"

"Listen up, big man," she said in a low voice. "Over the last week, I've stripped three bathrooms, taken up a thousand square feet of hardwood, disconnected dozens of electrical sockets and removed countless lights. If your point is that I'm a klutz or I don't know what I'm doing, you're dead wrong. The men have contusions and cuts, too. It's part of the job. A job I'm damn good at, by the way."

His eyes stared down at her, the irises so dark they were nearly black. She expected him to cut her to shreds with that sharp tongue of his and she was prepared to meet him head-on with some choice slices of her own.

Instead he stayed quiet until she was ready to jump out of her skin.

She couldn't stand it any longer.

"So are you canning me, or what?" she demanded. "Because if you aren't, you need to remember something. This is not your boat. I'm the boss here. If you can't handle that, then don't come into White Caps again until the project's finished."

His eyes narrowed even further and she thought he was going to kick her out on her butt, she really did. He was that angry.

And then all the emotion sucked out of his face, as if he'd opened a drain somewhere. The self-control struck her as eerie and intimidating.

He dropped her arm and stepped back. "I'm sorry."

She released the breath she'd been holding. "I don't take unnecessary risks. Truly. You don't have to worry about me."

"You're right. Because you're not my problem. Or my responsibility." He walked over to the door. "Thank you for reminding me."

As the plastic flap fell back into place behind him, Cass felt as if she'd been dropped at the side of the highway and abandoned. Which was nuts. She didn't appreciate his chest-thumping routine, so why should she feel let down when he cut it out?

Not my problem.

She closed her eyes.

Funny, what bothered her most was the reminder that he saw her as nothing more than an irritation. After the dinner they'd had, she'd thought she might have broken through to him just a little.

Clearly, she'd been wrong.

* * *

Alex forced himself to stay away from the house for the whole week. He figured it was a good idea to give them both a chance to cool down.

Cassandra was right, of course. It was her job, her crew, her profession. He had no right to stick his nose into her business. God knew, if someone had come onto his boat and tried to tell him what do, he'd have tossed them overboard in a heartbeat. All things considered, she'd handled the intrusion a lot better than he would have.

Especially given the number of power tools she'd had at her disposal.

The thing was, he hadn't been thinking clearly at the time. He'd gone down to the house because he'd been unable to stay away any longer and he was curious about what they were doing with the truck. He'd walked into the kitchen, caught a quick glimpse of her about five feet from that straining rope, and he'd totally lost it. What he'd wanted to do was take her into his arms, but that would have been inappropriate. So he'd yelled at her instead.

Something that was equally uncalled for.

The sound of truck engines turning over had him looking at his watch. Three o'clock. The men were leaving for the weekend.

Picking up his cane, he didn't bother with a coat as he headed for the door. He owed Cassandra a better apology than the one he'd given her and he needed to get the groveling over with.

As he hobbled down to the house, he pictured her rising up on tiptoe so she could meet him in the eye and keep arguing with him. Not many people fought to get closer to him when he was pissed off. His crew tended to duck and cover when his temper got pounding, and even Reese had backed away.

Cassandra's strength as she'd met him head-on had been a surprise. He'd always known she was lovely and smart, but had never considered her tough. Naturally, the hard edge turned him on even more. He could appreciate lovely. He could respect smart. But strong made him tingle all over.

As if his libido needed the help when it came to her.

When he got to the house, he pulled back the plastic sheet and stepped into the kitchen. Cassandra was bent over the propane heater, shutting it off.

"Hey."

She wheeled around, putting her hand to her throat. After a quick glance at his face, her eyes refused to meet his. "You scared me."

"Sorry."

"Have you come to check on our progress?" She picked up a clipboard, folded back a couple pages and made a note.

"No."

"Then why are you here?"

"I owe you an apology."

That got her attention. Her eyes shifted to his. "You mean for Monday? You already gave me one if memory serves."

"I was way out of line. I'm sorry."

She pulled on a parka, juggling the clipboard between her hands. "So you said. Are we done?"

He stepped in her path. "You're still angry."

"Yes, I am. Now get out of my way."

"Cassandra—"

"I am *not* a problem," she snapped.

"What the—what are you talking about?"

"As you left on Monday you said I wasn't your problem.

Well, you're right about the first part. I'm not your anything, not your friend, not your colleague, certainly not someone you need to worry about. But I'm also not a problem. I take care of myself, I always have, ever since I was sixteen. Hell, even while I was married to Reese, with all his money, I paid my own expenses. So I am *no* man's problem, got it?"

Alex dragged a hand through his hair. "Ah, hell—"

She propped her clipboard on her hip and leaned against some exposed wall studs. "You know, I'm curious. What exactly do you think is so awful about me? Just be honest. I mean, after I leave this job, I'm never going to see you again, so why don't we let it all out. I'd like to know why you've always disliked me."

Alex cursed, a low, vile word that made her laugh harshly.

"Not up to it?" she said in a brisk tone. "Funny, I always assumed you played honest. Big tough guy like yourself. Not afraid of anything."

"Damn it, woman, will you give me a minute to collect my thoughts?"

"Oh, so there's a list."

As he blew out his breath, she shook her head.

"God—" She stepped around him. "—Goddamn you, Alex."

He put his arm out, stopping her. "You've got it all wrong, Cassandra. About you and me."

"How so? Are you going to tell me you haven't avoided me all these years? That you haven't glowered every time you saw me on a dock waiting for the two of you to come in? You jumped ship to get away from me, remember? On that cruise through the Bahamas. You couldn't wait to get off that boat, and don't pretend I wasn't what drove you away."

Alex clamped down on his molars. He was an inch away from letting the whole sordid mess fly. His obsession, his love, his hunger. But it wouldn't be fair to burden her with all that. Like she needed to know he was crazed for her. And had…

Killed her husband.

He squeezed his eyes shut, not wanting her to read the sins in his stare.

"At least you don't deny it," she said softly.

He listened to her leave: the footsteps, the flapping of the plastic, the Range Rover's engine turning over.

He didn't open his eyes until he was all alone.

The next morning, on Saturday, Cass headed to the site. She was going back to Manhattan for the holidays early the following day and she wanted to put in another good bunch of hours before she left.

Plus she had a lot of frustration to work off.

As she got out of the Range Rover and walked over to the house, she didn't bother looking at the shop. She wasn't going to look at it again.

Not anymore.

For too long she'd been determined to bang her head against the wall that was Alex Moorehouse. And it was hard to own up to the fact that yesterday she really had wanted him to tell her she'd read him wrong. She'd honestly hoped he'd say there was no basis for what she believed was true.

When he hadn't been able to, she'd been stupidly hurt. Again.

Enough was enough. Alex's particular brand of disapproval triggered every need-to-please strand in her DNA. But they were going in circles and she wasn't a masochist. At least not an infinite masochist. She was giving up. Letting go.

Stamping a big *WHATEVER* on the situation and walking away.

She went into the house, turned the heater on, started the generator and headed upstairs. The bathrooms were essentially cleared out. All she wanted to do to them today was remove the molding around the windows and doors and take off the wainscoting on the walls. It was the perfect kind of small job for her. She just needed a hammer, a chisel for leverage and time.

She picked the biggest of the baths to begin with. After turning on a space heater, she took off her parka, put her bag of lunch down and started in the left-hand corner of the room. Finding a rhythm in her work was a blessing, and as it always was when she was alone at a site with nothing but boards and tools and quiet, the hours flew by. Toward the end of the day, she'd gotten so much done she thought she might as well take up some of the tile on the floor, as well.

The sun was setting when she decided to call it quits. Her shoulders were sore, her back stiff and the satisfaction of looking over the piles of boards she'd taken off wiped away all of the discomfort.

She'd done a good job. Made progress.

Downstairs, she shut off the propane heater and the generator. As she lifted the plastic to leave, the cold rushed in and reminded her that she'd left her parka up where she'd been working. She ran back to the bathroom and grabbed the jacket. Just as she was leaving, the scorched particleboard under her feet let out a shriek. She looked down at a section where she'd removed some tile.

It happened so fast. One moment she was fine, the next, her foot broke through the board and she was through the floor up to her thigh.

While she caught her breath, she waited for the pain to tell her what, if anything, had been broken. The dull thudding in her upper leg suggested she was going to be bruised, but she was able to move her foot, and there was no awful feeling of wetness as blood welled.

Thank God for her long underwear and her jeans. The two together had saved her from getting torn up.

Planting her palms on the floor, she tried to lift herself out of the hole and failed. After a day spent popping boards off the wall, her shoulder and back muscles were spent and she couldn't get much leverage, not with her free leg splayed out behind her. The layers she wore were also part of the problem. All that fabric was crammed into the hole, trapping her.

She eyed the window. The sun was almost down. What little heat there was in the house was evaporating quickly, the temperature dropping inside and out.

Taking a deep breath, she yelled, "Alex! Alex! Can you hear me?"

Chapter Eight

Alex looked up from the desk and frowned. Something was off. Something…

He cocked his head to the side, trying to loosen his neck. His nape was tingling as if someone were standing right behind him, even though he was by himself.

His witchy sense was kicking in, although damned if he knew why. He looked around the workshop. Everything was in order and his phone wasn't ringing with some kind of emergency.

Maybe it was just a draft.

As he bent his head the other way, he smiled a little. His crew hated whenever he started cricking his neck. Usually it meant trouble was coming. Or had arrived but just hadn't introduced itself yet.

He looked back down at the sailboat design he was working on. He'd finally decided to stop fighting the urge to play around with his father's old plans. And after having gone through all of them, he'd decided they were really good. With some tweaking, a few of them could be spectacular.

Sometime later he took a stretch and checked his watch. Seven o'clock. Time to eat again. He went over to the little refrigerator and started lining up the cans of Ensure. With those, plus the three chicken breasts he'd boiled that afternoon and some pre-washed lettuce he had, he'd pull down about twelve hundred calories. Not bad, but he was going to have to squeeze in a couple more PowerBars before he went to bed.

He was rubbing the back of his neck, annoyed by the persistent twitchy feeling, when his cell phone went off. He checked caller ID before answering.

"Hey, Libby. What's up?"

The older woman's voice was edgy. "Have you seen Cassandra?"

"Isn't she home with you?"

"She should have been. About two hours ago."

As his nape went into a crazy spasm, fear condensed in his chest cavity. He looked out the window at White Caps. The lights were off and he couldn't see where she parked her car from this vantage point.

"I'm going over to the house," he said. "I'll call you back."

He grabbed his parka, clicked on a flashlight and headed out as quickly as he could. The Range Rover was parked where it usually was, but there were no sounds from inside the house. The silence made the cold air seem so much colder.

Pulling back the plastic, he called out, "Cassandra?"

"Alex?" Her thin, ghostly voice drifted down to his ears.

He flipped the flashlight up. Her leg was dangling out of the kitchen ceiling.

"Cassandra!" Punching his cane into the floor, he went upstairs, cursing his cast and the way it slowed him down.

He found her in one of the bathrooms. In a space that was as frigid as the outdoors.

"Th-thank God." She shuddered. "Alex…"

Without nailing her eyes with direct light, he did a quick assessment of her. She had one leg stretched out behind her, the other through the floor up to her hip. A parka was wrapped loosely around her upper body, but it was so cold, the thing obviously wasn't doing much good. Her teeth were chattering, and the color was sucked out of her cheeks.

He kneeled down, carefully positioning his lower leg. "Does anything feel broken?"

"I can bend my knee a little. Ankle, foot and t-toes flex without pain. I think all the layers I'm w-wearing helped me from getting cut, too. I'm just not strong enough to p-pull myself free."

"Any problem with your spine?"

She shook her head. "I have f-feeling everywhere. Or I did before the c-cold took it away."

He put the flashlight down. "Okay, here's the plan. I'm going to grab you under your arms. I want your hands on my shoulders, but don't pull yourself up, let me do the work. You're going to go limp, understand? The less tense you are, the easier this will be. Any questions?"

Cassandra looked up at him. "You've rescued people b-before."

Yeah, but not like this. His hands were shaking so badly he had to hide them from her.

"Any questions?" he repeated.

"No," she said in a small voice.

He got close to her, slipped his hands under the parka

and gripped her body. God, she was so small. His palms spanned her rib cage.

"You ready?" he said into her ear.

"Alex?" she whispered.

"Don't worry, I'll go slow. I'm going to try not to hurt you."

"I'm glad you c-came. I was calling your n-name."

Squeezing his eyes shut, he took a deep breath. "Okay, honey. Here we go."

He called upon all the brute strength of his upper body, marshaling the heavy muscles of his shoulders and biceps to lift her weight. Her breath caught and she let out a groan. But she moved.

"How you doing?" he said through clenched teeth. His bad leg was screaming in pain, but he wasn't about to stop.

"F-fine. Thank you."

Alex eased back and she came with him until she was free. With a twist, he laid her out on the floor and stuffed her arms in her parka, zipping her inside. There was a brief silence between them as he leaned over her, breathing deeply, and she stared up at him, lying perfectly still.

He brushed a tendril of hair back from her face.

You are not going to kiss her, Moorehouse. Don't you dare.

His head dipped down. As she shivered, he pulled himself up short, appalled. He needed to get her the hell out of this house and warmed up. He did not need to waste time doing something he shouldn't do even when she was perfectly well.

"I want to check your leg before you try and stand on it, okay?"

She nodded, burrowing into her coat.

Keeping his hands impersonal, he ran them over her ankle and calf, bending the bones a little. She winced when he got to her thigh.

"How bad's the pain?"

"Just a bruise kind of thing. And, no, I don't need a doctor."

He tried to ignore the fact that his hand was way up on the inside of her leg, but the intimacy was too loud for him to drown it out. God, he was a bastard. The poor woman was freezing cold; he could feel her trembling. And he was thinking about sex?

Men truly are pigs, he thought.

"I don't feel anything," he said. Now, there was a lie. His body was on fire. "Let's get you out of here. Light-headed?"

She shook her head and sat up, pushing him away when he would have helped her. She awkwardly got to her feet and reached for the wall. As she swayed, he wondered how he was going to keep her upright when he had so little balance himself.

Except before he even got off the floor, Cassandra turned away and started for the stairs.

Alex palmed his cane, wondering why she'd rather go it on her own when it was clear she was so unsteady.

"I want to take you to Gray's," he called out while struggling to get up off the floor. "Cassandra! Wait!"

He caught her on the stairs only because she was taking them slowly.

"I'm taking you to Gray's," he said to her back.

"That's okay." She stumbled and caught herself on the banister. "It's not far."

The hell he was going to let her get behind the wheel. "I'll drive you."

"Not with that c-cast you won't. The Range Rover is a stick shift. Reese liked to t-trailer boats behind it."

"Why are you racing out of here? Will you—damn it, Cassandra! Stop."

They came into the kitchen. While she went for the clipboard and her cell phone, he headed to the door, blocking the exit.

As she came up to him, she looked right through him. "Pl-please get out of the w-way, Alex."

She was so cold her lips were blue.

He widened his stance. If she wanted out, she was going to have to break through him. "You're coming up to the shop. You're getting under the hot water. Then maybe I'll let you drive home. Otherwise, I'm calling Spike to come pick you up."

"Three words," she muttered.

"What?"

"Not. Your. Problem."

He cursed with a nasty, dark word. "There's no fricking way I'm letting you drive in this condition."

Her shoulders sagged. "I d-don't want to argue with you."

He took her arm. "Good. Let's go."

"Alex—"

"Now."

When she followed him past her car and up to the shop, he was relieved.

Once they were inside, he led her right over to his bed, forcing her down gently, getting her as close to the pot-bellied stove as he could. Moving quickly, he put some more wood on the fire and went into the bathroom. After the shower was running strong, he picked up the wet towel he'd used after his workout and shut the door so the room would warm up.

"Water should be ready in a minute." He tossed the towel into the laundry duffel and went over to the desk. He dialed Gray's.

"Libby?" he said when the woman answered. "I have her. She's fine. Just warming up. No, she's okay. She'll be home in a while."

He hung up and looked across the room.

Cassandra was shivering more now that she was out of the cold.

"Let's get your boots off," he said, going over to her. He leaned on his cane and lowered himself to her feet.

"I can do it." But when she reached down, her fingers skipped over the laces.

He removed her Timberlands, being careful with the one on the right. Then he stripped off her socks.

She had very pretty feet.

He curled his hand around her ankle and he felt the bones again, sliding his palm under her pant leg and up her calf. Her long johns prevented him from knowing how smooth her skin was. Which was just as well.

When she went dead still under his touch, he knew she was hiding something from him.

"Where's the pain?" he asked in a low voice. "Cassandra?"

He looked up. Her eyes were watching him from under lowered lids.

"Cassandra, where does it hurt?"

"It doesn't. Not really."

Yeah, right. Then why was she so motionless? "Look, I know you don't think you need a physician, but tomorrow you should go see Doc John."

"I'm driving back to Manhattan tomorrow. First thing in the morning."

He frowned. "Why?"

"The holidays."

"When will you be back?"

"Right after New Year's."

God, that was forever. "Do you need help getting to the bathroom?"

She shook her head and started to shrug out of her parka. Her hands were clumsy as she took it off and he eyed her flannel shirt. The thing was buttoned to the neck.

Instead of getting up and going to the desk, Alex nudged her hands aside.

"Let me do it," he said gruffly.

"No, I can—"

"Yeah, right." When she tried to bat him away, he muttered, "Don't worry, I've seen it all before."

That last comment was for him, not her. He couldn't believe he was about to take off her clothes.

She was silent as he worked on the flannel, which was just fine with him. Any conversation would have gone nowhere because he was using all his focus to keep his hands from shaking as badly as hers were. Especially as he went for the button between her breasts.

Even though she was wearing a turtleneck under the shirt, he imagined he was seeing her with nothing on. The idea of all that creamy skin...

Her breath caught and he flicked his eyes to her face. She was watching his fingers.

He tugged the shirt free of her waistband and undid the last three buttons. Then he slowly slid the flannel from her shoulders. Now he didn't look at her face. He couldn't. His body was alive, the heat tightening his gut, hardening him.

He didn't want her to know it.

"I can get the turtleneck," she said roughly.

He nodded. "How about your pants?"

"I'm sure I'll figure a way—"

"Button-fly, aren't they? So let me do it." When she didn't say anything, he reached for the waistband. The top fastening came free easily. So did the next. And the one after that. And the fourth. And the final.

The jeans parted, revealing a thick pair of red long johns.

Alex swallowed and gripped the belt loops. "Lift your hips."

Her body shifted, her breasts rising. He should only have drawn the jeans off her, but he hooked his thumbs under the waist of the long johns, too. He took it all down, moving over her thighs and her knees, tracing each inch of flesh that he exposed with his eyes.

Her panties were white silk.

He looked away, knowing he was about to fall on her like a starving man.

"Water'll be warm now," he said in a clipped voice as he folded up what he had removed. "I'll give you my back for the rest. That bathroom's too small to undress in, trust me."

He struggled off the floor and limped over to the desk. When he sat down, he tried to look at the plans he'd been reworking. And could have been staring at a blank wall for all they held his attention.

As he heard the bed springs creak softly, he looked into the window and caught the reflection of her standing up. She gripped the edge of the turtleneck and slowly lifted it up and over her head as if she were stiff.

Alex saw her breasts in profile, the gentle swells covered with wisps of silk. He told himself to shut his eyes but couldn't as her hands moved to the front of her bra and released a catch. With an arch that pushed taut tips out, she took the thing off and let it drop to the mattress. Then she slid her thumbs under the waistband of her panties and took them down to the floor.

He swallowed a groan. And watched her coil her hair up and tie it in place.

When she disappeared into the bathroom, Alex cursed himself, his body hard as the wooden chair he was sitting in.

He told himself he was going to stay right where he was.

Over and over again.

Chapter Nine

Cass stepped under the hot spray, craning her neck so the water hit her face and ran down her body. She was trembling, but not from the cold.

From Alex.

She was so pathetic. He'd been nothing but clinical in the way he'd touched her, especially while undressing her. But the sight of his long fingers unbuttoning her shirt and then her pants... His dark head lowered, the clean smell of him so close... She'd wanted to lie back on that bed and pull him on top of her.

Cass closed her eyes. Yeah, that was a good plan. Exactly what someone did when they were letting a man go. Right. Sure.

Except, she knew he would feel so perfect against her. He would be warm and heavy, those muscles shifting as he loved her body with his own.

From out of the past, she had a sudden image of him stepping naked from that bathroom on the boat—

Oh, dear Lord.

Her eyes popped open and she squeezed her arms around herself.

Oh, no.

She wanted him. And it wasn't just now. She had…wanted him for a long time.

It had started on that trip. That trip she and Reese had taken with him to the Bahamas. That trip when she'd caught him in the cabin by mistake. She'd gone below deck to get a drink, thinking she and Reese were alone on the boat. Alex had emerged from the bathroom, beautifully naked, droplets of water clinging to the smooth skin of his back. He'd looked over his shoulder, his tattoo shifting as he did, his eyes narrowing as he'd caught her red-handed.

He must have seen something in her face that day. And that was why he'd left the boat at the next port.

No wonder the guy didn't want her around. Alex had honor. He wouldn't stand for being ogled by his best friend's wife.

Oh…hell.

Although, it wasn't as if she would ever have acted on her attraction. She'd taken her wedding vows very seriously, all of them. But Alex couldn't have known that.

Opening her eyes, she looked at the soap and the shampoo he used. As she pictured him standing naked where she was, she knew she had to get back to Gray's right away.

She was so much better off being angry at Alex, she thought. Because now, after she'd spent two hours in the cold, and then been rescued by the man, she was feeling vulnerable. And vulnerable was not good, not around him.

When she got out of the shower, she looked around for a towel and couldn't find one. She cracked the door open a little. Alex was sitting at his desk, bent over sailboat plans. She noticed he'd taken off the cast.

"Excuse me, Alex?"

"Yeah?" His voice was not encouraging.

"Do you have a towel I could use?"

She thought she heard him curse under his breath as the chair was pushed back.

He went to the duffels on the floor, pulled a navy blue square from one of them, and snapped it so it unfolded. She put her hand out, expecting him to throw the thing over.

Instead he brought it to her.

"Thanks. I'll get out of your hair—"

She pulled on the towel a little. He didn't let go.

Her eyes lifted to his. "Alex?"

He said nothing.

A long silence stretched out between them, and she had the vague sense they were on the brink of something.

"Alex?"

He didn't answer her. Instead, he pushed the door open with his shoulders and came into the bathroom, holding the towel up to her body. As he shut them in together, she squeezed back into the shower stall because it was either that or she would be on him like another set of clothes.

Mist swirled around as he let her take hold of the towel. Then he reached up and pulled her hair out of the knot she'd put it in.

"Alex," she whispered. "What are you doing?"

He lifted his hand and cupped her chin. In a slow sweep, his thumb brushed over her lower lip.

Her body came alive, heat scorching her bones, incinerating common sense. She stared up at him, unable to move as he loomed over her. His face was impassive, made of stone, but she could sense the coiled need in him, the powerful sexual drive churning in his blood.

His thumb pressed into her mouth, penetrating her as he tightened his hold on her chin. He pushed in and out, caressing her, taking her, and her body responded as if it were his hips, not his thumb, her core, not her mouth. She swayed, breath leaving her in a rush, her heart pounding.

A feeling of total dislocation overcame her. She couldn't understand how he'd ended up in the bathroom with her. Why he was touching her as he was. How this change had occurred.

But there were two things she didn't question. His need. Her response.

"Do you want this?" he asked roughly.

"This" was crazy. Confusing. A total turnaround for him and a revelation for her. But yes, she did, she wanted him.

Cass replied the only way she could. She pulled her lips in tight and sucked his finger.

With a low growl, he slid his thumb from her mouth and leaned forward. Her lips parted, but at the last moment he veered to the side and found her neck. His teeth closed gently on the side of her throat and then he licked where he'd nipped her. Her head fell back as his strong arms wound around her and pulled her against him.

He was so tall he had to bend down to stay at her throat, and she bowed with him. She felt the broad expanse of his chest against hers. His hard belly. His thighs.

And between his legs, his thick arousal.

She was shocked that he wanted her. But then his hands

started moving over her and she stopped thinking. His lips nibbled their way down to her collarbone, traveling, nuzzling. She grabbed on to his shoulders.

"Cassandra," he said against her shoulder. "If you don't tell me to stop, right now, I'm going to finish this."

His voice was totally level. She didn't know how he managed it. She was starting to pant.

Did she want this to happen? she thought. Was she ready to make love with someone else?

With Alex, of all people?

His hands dipped to her hips and squeezed, sending a lash of heat to the very core of her. Going on instinct, she wrapped a leg around one of his, rubbing herself against him. He groaned, a low rumble in his chest, and pulled back.

"Tell me to stop, Cassandra, or I'm going to take you to that bed outside."

She hesitated. And then whispered, "So take me."

He seemed to pale, as if her answer was the last one he'd expected. But then he opened the door. The rush of cool air cleared out most of the mist and did nothing for her brain. She was still floating in crazed disbelief, the whole experience having the hazy patina of a dream.

"Do you have any protection?" he asked.

Now that fazed her. Brought some reality into the dim room.

"Um, no, I don't. But I'm not… I'm clean." She hadn't been with anyone since Reese. And after she'd found out he was cheating, she hadn't made love with him, either. That was two years ago. But there was another aspect to safe sex, wasn't there? "And I…I won't get pregnant."

"They tested me for everything when I was in the hospital."

She gripped the edge of the towel. The implications of what they were going to do were suddenly very clear. Too clear. She backed away.

Alex followed, coming up to her and putting his hands to her face. His expression was harsh, but he was so very gentle as he sank his fingers into her hair and fanned it out along her shoulders. His eyes traced the waves as if he were memorizing how they looked. Then his head tilted down.

Giving up the fight, she opened her mouth, ready for his kiss, but he went for her earlobe, sucking on it, catching it between his teeth and tongue. He moved her around slowly until she felt something hit the backs of her calves. The bed. She let herself fall onto the mattress, and he eased himself down so he was lying side by side with her. There really wasn't enough space for them both, and his thigh moved up over her legs so he didn't fall off. The weight was daunting. And delicious.

She let go of the towel and found the lip of the fleece he was wearing. Sliding her hand inside, she felt hard muscle and soft skin. He surged at the contact, his legs shifting as he suddenly rolled on top of her. She parted for him, embracing him with her thighs.

His lips drifted down to the edge of the towel. With hands that shook, he pulled the thing off her and pitched it to the floor.

Alex stared at her breasts for so long she wondered if there was something wrong with them. When she lifted her hands to cover herself, he shook his head and pressed his lips to the valley at her sternum. His hand drifted up and caressed her, narrowing in until the tips of his fingers passed over one taut nipple. She gasped and arched and his mouth latched on to her, suckling, tugging sweetly.

Pleasure broke and she dragged her hands through his thick hair. His hips drove forward, his hardness pressing into her through his jeans, and then he moved to the side. His palm swept down her belly and on to her hip. When it moved to the inside of her thigh, the nerves kicked in.

They were moving so fast. It was all happening so—

He found where she ached, touching her delicately with his big hand. As she shuddered from the heat, she looked up into his face. His eyes were closed, his expression rapt.

Without asking, he knew how she liked to be stroked and parted and circled. It wasn't long before she was crying out his name, trembling in the throes of the sensations he gave her. She gripped him and threw her head back, the pulsating release coming up on her fast and lingering for a long time.

When she drifted back into her body, she opened her eyes. Alex was looking down at her. Remote.

She frowned, wondering if she'd turned him off with her intensity. It had sure surprised her. She glanced down his body. No, he was definitely still aroused. But he was motionless.

"Alex? Are you...do you want to..."

For a crushing moment she thought he was going to leave. But then he shifted and she heard a zipper.

When he mounted her, the blunt feel of him brushing against her core made her dizzy, and her whole body tingled with anticipation. He entered her slowly, inching inside, a thick presence that took up all her inner space. When their hips met, he paused.

His body trembled so badly, the bed frame rattled.

"Alex? Are you okay?"

His arms came around her as he buried his head in her neck. He pulled back and then gently slid inside again.

She latched on to his shoulders, holding on tight, as sensation built inside of her again. The feel of him was incredible, his heavy weight, that hard length, his slow, flowing movements.

But then he stopped, and withdrew abruptly.

He got off the bed and turned away, doing up his pants.

Seeing him fully clothed while she was naked kicked off a cold tidal wave in her veins and illuminated some particulars that she'd missed.

He hadn't kissed her. He hadn't even been naked with her.

And he hadn't been able to finish.

Cassandra was dressed and out the door in a minute and a half.

The fact that he didn't stop her, didn't say a word, wasn't a surprise. He hadn't talked to her during the sex, either. Except for that clinical safety conversation.

Had they even had sex?

She ran to the Range Rover, fired the thing up and threw it in reverse. As she hit the gas, she realized she'd left her cell phone and clipboard in the shop.

Yeah, like she was going back in there tonight.

As the Rover's headlights swung around, they pierced the picture window. Alex was sitting at the desk, head in his hands.

He looked as if he were...sobbing.

She was so struck by his utter dejection, her foot eased up on the gas.

But then it hit her.

Of course he feels awful, she thought.

He'd just cheated on his Miracle woman, the one he loved, hadn't he?

Alex didn't know how long he sat in the chair, blinking back tears he refused to let fall.

Crying wasn't only a worthless thing to do. It was another kind of self-serving release he refused to let himself have.

Oh, God…had that really just happened? Had he truly done that to her?

Yes, he thought. He could still smell her glorious passion on him.

It had been so wrong of him. And felt so perfect.

Her body was even more beautiful than his dreams had made it out to be, and her skin was even softer, especially where her hot secrets were kept. When she'd flown apart in his arms, he'd watched her with greed, thinking this was what he had always wanted. His name coming out of her lips because of what he was doing to her.

For those few moments he'd joined them, he'd known paradise. She was so very tight that every stroke had been a revelation of ecstasy, like nothing he'd ever had, nothing he'd find again. Pulling back from her had nearly killed him. He'd been right in the very beginnings of a shattering release, the pulses just starting to take his breath away, when he'd stopped.

Because how could he empty himself into her body, knowing what he did? It would be tantamount to violating her, because she would deny him if she knew the truth.

From somewhere in the shop, a cell phone rang. The tone wasn't his.

He looked up. She'd left hers behind. Forgotten it along with the clipboard in her rush to leave.

Dear Lord, what she must think of him. And how she must feel, to have been left on the bed like that. He should do something.

Except, what were his options? What could he say to her to make things better?

I stopped because you deserve so much better than a savage like me coming inside of you.

The phone fell silent, only to ring again. On the fourth round of chiming, he went over and flipped it open.

Before he could say a word, a male voice blasted into his ear.

"Cass, what's wrong? That message you just left sounded damned scary."

O'Banyon.

Alex went cold.

"Hello?" O'Banyon said.

"She's at Gray's."

There was a long silence and then that male voice dropped down a register. "Why do you have Cass's phone, Moorehouse?"

"She left it at the site." Which was technically true. "Do you have Gray's number?"

"Do you know why she was crying tonight?"

Ah…hell. Alex dragged a hand through his hair.

"What the hell did you do to her?" O'Banyon snarled.

"Do you have Gray's number?"

"So help me God, Moorehouse, I'm not going to allow you to grind her up. I'll come north tonight and drag her back to Manhattan if I have to."

"Suit yourself, O'Banyon. I won't stand in your way. Now, if you don't mind, I'm going to hang up on you and turn this phone off. Your voice in my ear is nothing I want to fall asleep to."

After he'd shut the cell down, Alex went straight for the scotch bottle and poured himself a tall one. He was halfway through it when he picked up his phone and called Spike.

"Hey, man, what's doing?" the guy said.

"I need a favor."

"Anything."

"Could you come by tomorrow morning early? Cassandra left her cell phone and her clipboard at the site. She's leaving to go back to the city and she'll want to take them with her."

"No problem. But why can't she just pick them up herself on the way out of town?"

"She's not going to want to be here for a little while." Alex took a long drink. The scotch burned its way down to his gut.

"Why?"

"You ever done something you wished you could undo?"

Spike laughed softly. "You better believe it."

"Well, she's done something she wishes she hadn't, you know what I mean? I want to make it easy for her."

There was a long pause. "So it's like that, is it?"

Alex finished the glass. "Yeah. And then some."

Spike let out a long exhale. "I'll see you bright and early in the a.m."

"Thanks."

Alex put the glass down and eyed the bed. He stripped naked, letting his clothes fall where they chose to, and threw back the sheets and blankets. As he stretched out, he could smell her scent on his pillow.

Chapter Ten

On New Year's Eve, Cass hit the directional signal and eased the Range Rover off the Northway and onto the Saranac Lake exit. Her time away from White Caps had gone by fast, but it had done her some good. When she'd left before Christmas, she'd been raw. Now she was just bruised.

"So, Cass, tomorrow's your birthday, isn't it?" Sean said, glancing across the seats. "New Year's Day."

Sean had proved to be a godsend over the holidays. He'd insisted she come to his place for all of Christmas day. His brother, Billy, had been there as well, visiting from their hometown of Boston, and the three of them had had a great time. Billy was a linebacker for the New England Patriots, and considering his size, he no doubt lived up to his nickname of Boneyard on the field. But around her he'd been a total gentleman.

And so had Sean.

"Cass?"

She smiled. "Yes, I'll be thirty-one tomorrow."

As they passed by the stone pillars that marked the White Caps driveway, her eyes lingered on them.

Sean cleared his throat. "Why won't you tell me what happened that night you called me?"

"Oh, it was nothing. I was just a little emotional."

"Over Moorehouse."

"Sean—"

"I talked to him."

Cass's head whipped around so fast the car wobbled in their lane. "Alex?"

"None other. I called you on your cell first. Eventually he answered it."

"What did he say?"

"Not much. But his tone of voice had been exactly like yours."

Yeah, well, regret sounded the same, no matter whose mouth it was coming out of.

"Sean, I'm telling you, everything is fine."

There was a pause. And then he said, "You and I are getting close. Right?"

She smiled. "You're a good friend."

"Damn straight. And I'd like to be more, except I know you don't feel that way about me."

"Oh, Sean—"

"Nah, don't apologize for it. It's better this way. I've got plenty of lovers, but I've never actually had a girl-friend before. Anyway, my point is, don't lie to me. You shouldn't have to, and frankly I take it as an insult."

"Honestly, there's nothing going on."

Sean let out a disgusted noise, but he let the fib stand.

Cass pulled into Gray's driveway. There were ten or so cars parked around the gravel circle and she was forced to take a spot right in front of the door. Lights glowed in the mansion's diamond paned windows, and she could see people moving inside. She wondered which of the shadows was Alex's.

She really didn't feel up to the house party. Or being under the same roof with him again.

She turned off the engine and glanced at Sean. His hazel eyes were shrewd but warm. And that stare of his was seeing all the things she'd tried to hide behind makeup and haute couture.

"Cass, you should stay away from Moorehouse. That 'nothing' with him is killing you."

Sean really didn't miss much, did he?

And he truly was handsome, she thought, in a tough kind of way. Sure, his clothes were civilized; the black suit and the icy-white button-down and the red tie were very Wall Street/old school banker. But with his midnight hair and his hard jaw, his wide shoulders and long legs, Sean O'Banyon was all hot-blooded man underneath the gloss.

She took a deep breath.

He smelled good, too. Expensive cologne.

He was also uncomplicated. With him there was no baggage. No awkwardness. No on-the-ledge, about-to-fall-off feeling.

"Why can't I be attracted to you?" she wondered aloud.

His eyes flared. "Well…you could give me a try. You know, find out."

Cass focused on his lips. They were beautifully made and a perfect deep pink color. As they parted a little, she caught the bright flash of his front teeth.

"If you want to kiss me," he said quietly, "I'm more than ready for it."

Lord help her, she leaned into him, tilted her head to the side and pressed her mouth to his.

She felt the rush of his breath going in fast, heard the hissing sound as it shot into his lungs. His body went rigid and shifted, as if he'd pushed his arms into the leather seat. She stroked his mouth a few times for good measure, trying to feel something, anything.

But it was pleasant. Nothing more.

Not what it had been like with Alex.

Cass pulled back.

Oh, what did she know? Alex had never actually put his mouth on hers.

Sean cleared his throat. "You really know how to kiss, woman. I can't feel my toes."

She laughed, appreciating his attempt to lighten things up. But when she looked at him, his stare was dead serious.

"You make me wish I were the man you really wanted." He opened the car door. "Moorehouse is a fool."

Alex stared out of the window in the living room, watching Cassandra kiss O'Banyon. The man was totally turned on; it was obvious in the way his eyes were shut and his body braced.

Alex glanced down at the floor, expecting to find his internal organs on it.

"Here's your drink, Moorehouse," Gray said. "What are you staring at—hey! Cass and SOB are here. Excellent."

Bennett took off for the front door.

Alex tossed the scotch back. Then tortured himself by

looking toward the foyer and waiting for the happy couple to come inside.

It seemed appropriate that a chilling breeze followed them into the house.

Oh, terrific, the guy was carrying her. And not in a big hurry to put her down as their hosts came up to greet them.

There was a swell of laughter as Cass pointed to her high heels and Sean lowered her to the floor. Tonight, she was dressed in full Manhattan socialite armor: a sleek black pantsuit with ropes of big pearls linked around her neck. At her side O'Banyon was looking a little flushed, no doubt from what had happened back in the car, not the over-the-threshold routine. His big smile was grating as hell.

As more people stepped forward to say hello to the new arrivals, Alex stayed back, wishing he could leave. Spike was into the party, though, talking with a knot of women in the corner. And the guy's car was a stick.

Cassandra was laughing when she turned and saw him.

Her smile faltered, and the red splash that hit her cheeks was clearly shame, not delight, because it was backed up by a wince. She looked away quickly, not acknowledging him, but O'Banyon caught the exchange. He pegged Alex with a pair of hazels that read BACK OFF loud and clear. Then the man stepped in close and fit his arm around her waist.

Alex could understand the reaction. If Cassandra were his woman, he'd send the same message to any man who eyed her.

A meaty hand clapped on his shoulder, and Spike spoke right in his ear. "Do yourself a favor tonight, my man. Be careful with O'Banyon. This situation's got jaws of life written all over it."

Alex nodded. "I agree with you completely."

* * *

An hour later Cass was in total party numb. Too many people, too much noise, too little air.

Making an excuse to Jack Walker, the new governor of Massachusetts, she snuck out of the living room. She was surprised at the number of guests and partially grateful. The more bodies in the house, the harder it was to concentrate on Alex.

Well, not really.

She found herself always watching him out of the corner of her eye, seeing who he talked to and how he acted. He didn't seem any more interested in the party than she was. The only time he smiled was when Spike shot him a couple of words and a dry grin. Otherwise, Alex was a tall, silent presence that commanded people's attention even though he rarely opened his mouth.

Predictably, the women were captivated by him. They came up to him all the time, smiling, getting in tight, touching his arm, his shoulder. He barely noticed. He looked over their heads or through them, even when they got really persistent.

Unlike Spike he clearly wasn't taking any of the lovelies home tonight.

It was so different from the way Reese had behaved. Even when she'd been with her husband at a party, Reese had engaged in social sex. He'd been a toucher, a looker, a flirter, walking the line between sensuous and sleazy perfectly. Women had adored him and he'd adored them right back.

Alex, on the other hand, was choosy about who he shared himself with.

Cass grimaced, thinking of how he'd withdrawn from her body. Yes, he was definitely choosy.

Pushing her hair back, she uttered a vicious little word. She hadn't been able to forget their brief time on his bed and not just because of her embarrassment. The preoccupation struck her as unfair. How could it be so right on one side and so wrong for the other person?

And why had he been so aroused in the first place? Men couldn't lie about that.

Maybe she just looked like his Miracle.

Oh, there was a lovely thought.

Cass walked down the hall and went through a closed door into a library. Like the rest of Gray's house, the room was done up with antiques and damask drapes and Oriental rugs. But that wasn't what recommended the space to her. Quiet was its main attraction.

Across the way there were a bank of windows that faced the water. She went over to them and took in the winter landscape. Snow covered the rolling lawn, a blanket that glowed blue in the moonlight. Farther down, the vast, frozen expanse of the lake stretched out between its cradle of mountains, flat as could be.

Voices broke her solitude as two women walked in, one blond, the other with sable-colored hair. Both were dressed in Soho black: close-cut, dark clothes made by obscure designers. If memory served, the blonde was an editor for *Vanity Fair* and her friend worked at *Town & Country.* Or maybe it was the other way around.

"I can't believe Alex Moorehouse is here," the blonde said. "I would love to do a story on him. Tragic champion and all that."

"I like his friend. Did you see those tattoos on his neck? I wonder how far down they go."

"Allison, your last four boyfriends had roman numerals

after their last names. That guy doesn't even *have* a sur-name. Spike? I mean, really."

"Did you see his eyes? They're yellow."

"I was too busy staring at Moorehouse. I wonder what it would take to open him up. Maybe he needs a ride home."

The two of them noticed her.

"Do you know if there is a bathroom around here?" the one named Allison asked.

Cass nodded to a door in the corner. "I think it's through there."

"You first," the blonde said to Allison. Then she turned and smiled at Cass. "My name's Erica Winsted, we met at the Hall Foundation Gala last year, remember? You know, I was sorry to hear about your husband."

"Thank you."

Erica did a little pirouette. "What a fabulous party this is. When Allison suggested we fly up, I thought she was crazy. But the people here? First-rate."

Chatty was about the last thing Cass felt up to. "If you'll excuse me—"

"Say, you wouldn't be willing to introduce me to Alex Moorehouse, would you? I'm dying to get to him. And he was your husband's partner, right?"

Cass just stared at the woman. Reporters really were awful, she thought.

Erica smiled. "I mean, you know him, right?"

"No, not at all."

The woman frowned as Cass walked out.

By a stroke of dumb luck, the stairs were right there and Cass used them with relief, heading up away from the party. She wasn't a coward to run to her room, she just needed a little space.

At least until the urge to lob a crepe at that reporter faded.

On the top landing there was a bench, and she sat on it, taking a deep breath. The party noise was dimmed only slightly, but it was enough to take the edge off and she found she liked watching the people funnel through the hall down below.

Until she heard, "Alex! Alex Moorehouse."

Alex came into view, and she caught the darkening of his expression.

The blond reporter came up to him and stuck her hand out. "Hi! I'm Erica Winsted. I'm such a huge fan of yours. All those races. I watch them religiously."

Alex looked at the woman from his height advantage. When he stayed silent, Erica plowed ahead.

"Listen, I would love to interview you."

"I'm sorry," he said, "what was your name?"

"Winsted. Erica Winsted. I write for—"

"Erica, I don't do interviews. Not now, not ever."

"Couldn't you make an exception for me?" She sidled up to him, moving her body closer to his.

Cass stiffened, imaging how Reese would have welcomed that kind of attention with a charming joke and an arm slipped around the woman's waist.

Alex stepped back pointedly. "Not for you. Sorry."

"Are you sure?"

God, you could practically hear the woman's eyelashes bat, Cass thought.

"Excuse me," Alex murmured, turning away.

"When are you going back to the boats?" Erica said. "When's your next race?"

Alex looked over his shoulder. "That's none of your business."

Cass frowned as he disappeared from sight.

She'd never thought about him going back. But of course he would. His leg was healing, and sailing was his profession.

The idea left her cold, even as she told herself it was none of her concern.

But, dear Lord, that hungry, scary ocean. That vast graveyard for sailors.

"Hey, beautiful. What's doing?"

She glanced down. Sean was at the foot of the stairs, leaning on the banister. He held out his hand. "Let me get you some dessert and coffee. Fireworks are going off at midnight and we don't want you to miss them on your birthday. Especially if Gray manages to toss the lit punk into the roman candle box. Like he did last year."

Cass smiled and went to him. As her palm slid into his, she said, "Sean, you're a nice guy, you know that?"

"Shh. Keep it to yourself. Nice guys get eaten alive on Wall Street."

Chapter Eleven

Sean O'Banyon liked to believe he had a talent for accurately assessing people. Aggressive men such as himself in particular.

So as he eyed Moorehouse from across the dining room, he knew the two of them were going to go at it tonight. Ever since he'd walked into the mansion with Cass, he and that hard-eyed athlete had been circling each other like a couple of wolves.

Cass stepped in front of him, pressing a coffee cup into his hand. "Sean?"

He smiled down at her. "What?"

"What's going on?"

"Nothing."

"Then why do you look like you want to wipe the floor with someone?"

He bent down and kissed her on the cheek. "Nothing for you to worry about."

She gave him a level look. "I'm going to go find Joy, okay? Try and stay out of trouble."

The moment she left, he pegged Moorehouse with a hard look that was returned pound for pound.

Time to get this over with, he thought, putting the coffee down.

Moorehouse must have come to the same conclusion because the guy started heading around the table from the other side. They met head-to-head in front of the dessert tray. Just as someone called out that the fireworks were about to go off down at the shore.

"You got a problem there, Moorehouse?" Sean asked as the room cleared.

"No more than you do." Moorehouse's sizable shoulders moved back, his unblinking eyes steady as a cobra's.

Man, he was a big one, Sean thought with satisfaction. This was going to be fun.

"You know," Sean said, "Cass left here a week ago feeling like hell. But as soon as she was back in Manhattan her mood improved. I wonder why?"

"None of my business."

Sean laughed and slipped the buttons on his suit jacket free.

"Well, wouldn't you know. You and I agree on something." He tapped his temple with his forefinger. "But see, this is where I get confused. You've been staring at me all night like maybe you and I have something going. Except considering that Cass is not your woman, I can't figure out why you're bothering. Unless you like the color of my eyes or something."

"I don't like much about you."

"Why's that?"

"You know your reputation as well as I do."

"Ah. Don't approve of my working-class background, do you?"

"How many lovers have you got going right now, O'Banyon? In addition to her, I mean?"

"So protective," Sean murmured. "You clearly think of yourself as her champion in some twisted way, don't you? Like it's okay for you to treat her badly, but no one else can, is that it?"

Moorehouse's blue eyes narrowed. "Careful, O'Banyon, reading other people's minds can be a real buzz kill."

"So can making a good woman cry. Or do you get off on it? Did you feel good, making her hurt like that?"

"Just so we're clear," Moorehouse said evenly, "the next insult you throw's coming back at your jaw."

Cass gasped.

The sound she made brought the men's heads around to the doorway. The effect was like a bell ringing in a boxing match. The two of them broke apart, Alex going over to the window, Sean dragging a hand through his hair and turning toward her.

"What is going on here?" she demanded.

"Just talking." Sean smiled and sauntered over to her, not that she bought his easy stride or lazy expression for a nanosecond. "Let's go watch the fireworks."

She glanced across the room. Alex's body was totally still as he stared out of the glass.

"Come on, Cass. The fireworks."

Alex's head dropped down.

"Leave us," she said to Sean. When he hesitated, she looked him right in the eye. "Go. Now."

When he'd left, she demanded, "You want to tell me what that was all about?"

"It was nothing."

God, men. "I want you to leave Sean alone."

Alex laughed tightly. "I think he can take care of himself. Now you better run along. He's waiting for you."

"What *is* your problem?"

There was a long silence and then he shrugged. "Do you think if I go and screw a bunch of women, I'll feel better, too? I mean, is working out your grief through men helping you?"

Cass narrowed her eyes. That was one hell of a cheap shot, she thought. As well as dead wrong.

"This coming from you?" she bit out. When he frowned over his shoulder, she put her hands on her hips. "Does your woman know about what happened between you and me?"

"What the hell are you talking about?"

"Your Miracle. The woman you love." As Alex paled, she shook her head. "What? You didn't think I knew? I heard you talking about her. That night Gray and Joy were married when I…came back for the plate."

Alex spun back to the window. And grabbed on to the sill as if steadying himself. "I thought that— I thought that was a dream."

His voice cracked at the end and the achy pitch softened her temper just a little. Boy, this situation between them was just so screwed up. On both ends.

"Where is she, Alex? Why isn't she here with you?"

He didn't answer, just propped his head up with his hand.

"Alex, why were you with me? You love her, right?"

Silence stretched out and then in a deadened voice, he said, "I am obsessed. She is like no other woman."

Cass's chest went cold, but she pressed on. "So why aren't you with your Miracle?"

"It can't work between us."

"She's not in your life?"

"Not the way I wish she was. Not the way...I want her. It would be inappropriate."

"How long have you—"

"Very long. I've loved her for years."

Years? Did he say years?

"Who is she?" Cass breathed, not that she expected him to tell her. "And if you feel so strongly, why did you take me to bed that night?" She slashed a hand through the air. "Wait—actually, don't answer that."

She already knew the *why* of it. He was a healthy male. She had been naked in his bathroom and really unresisting. Do the math.

God, she had to get away from him.

"Good night, Alex." She was almost out the door when pride made her say, "One last thing, though. I am not working out my grief through men. There is nothing going on between Sean and me."

"Liar," Alex said calmly.

Cass's mouth fell open as she stared at his broad back. "How dare you."

"I saw you in the car with him tonight. That was not friends. At least not in my book."

If his condemnation were any louder or more clear, she thought, it would have fireworks of its own.

She threw up her hands. "Why do you care what I do? Or who I'm with? What's it to you?"

"I want you." The words were spoken softly. Into the window, not at her.

"I'm so sick of this— What did you say?"

He wheeled around and came at her faster than she expected, his big body moving with only a slight lurch as he used his cane. Up close, she saw that his eyes were almost all black, they had dilated so completely.

"I want you. *Now.*" He looked to the doorway. "I want to shut us in here and get you under my body and take you, with all the people just outside. I want to strip your clothes off and put you on that table. Or lay you out on the floor. Or push you up against this wall."

He leaned to the side and splayed his hand out, as if testing the thing for strength.

She stared at him, stunned, until his eyes slid back to hers. Then she shook herself.

"Are you insane, Alex? As much as it kills me to point this out, you didn't like it with me, remember? It was a disaster. You couldn't even kiss me. You couldn't…finish. I was so humiliated when I left. God, I felt awful." Abruptly, a bone-deep weariness hit her, making her want to burst into tears. "Look, I don't know what kind of game you're playing, but I'm not up to it. Just leave me alone, okay?"

When she turned away, he took her hand, stopping her.

"Cassandra. Look at me. Please, just…look at me."

She glanced over her shoulder. "Why? So you can—"

"I'm so sorry about the way I left things with you." The anguish in his voice stilled her. And as if he recognized her change in mood, he reached out and stroked her cheek with his knuckles. "That night… It wasn't that I didn't want to…you know. I did. God, I really did."

"Alex—"

"It just felt unfair to you."

Unfair to her...?

Oh, right.

Cass closed her eyes. "So you were thinking of her the whole time, is that it? And that's why you wanted me. I must look like her, huh?"

His eyes traced over her face, her hair, her body. "You are no substitute."

Ah, yes. Because Miracle was perfection, Cass thought.

Okay, she really had to get out of here. Her self-esteem was getting cut to ribbons. Next on the hit parade would be bursting into tears in front of him. And wouldn't that be a terrific way to start her birthday?

"Let me go," she whispered, pulling at his grip.

He only tugged her closer.

"That night, all I saw was your hair on my pillow. Your skin in the dim light. Your beautiful, beautiful body. All I heard were the gasping sounds you made deep in your throat. Do you know what it did to me to hear you moan like that?" His voice became a low growl as he leaned down and spoke into her ear. "I want to go back there, Cassandra. Back to where I was with you. I want to taste you. I want your mouth under mine. I want to kiss your secrets. It's all about you."

Cass swayed, clinging to his arm. She didn't understand him, but she didn't doubt him. He was a lot of things, but never a liar.

And she wanted the same thing he did.

Oh...hell, it was happening again. Her rational thoughts were getting sucked under by her body's instinct to bring him inside.

What a perfect recipe for disaster, she thought. More sex with a man who had proven capable of hurting her over and over again.

Was she insane?

She looked at his lips. "Prove that I'm really the one you want tonight. Kiss me."

He stared at her long and hard. Then he murmured something that sounded like *I'm such a bastard.*

Before she could ask what he meant, his lips came down lightly on hers. They were soft as suede, brushing, stroking, so very gentle. And they trembled. In fact his whole body trembled, making her feel both precious and powerful.

He kissed her delicately for the longest time, sipping and teasing. When his tongue finally licked for permission to enter her mouth, she opened for him.

As he slid inside, he groaned. So did she.

He tasted like scotch and man and need. She smelled his aftershave, felt the hard muscles of his chest against her breasts, his flat belly tight on her own, his thighs.

His hard arousal, thick and straining.

Yes, she thought, sliding her hands around to his hips and bringing him closer. Oh, yes.

Dimly she heard the fireworks go off. Alex lifted his head.

"Cassandra…" He was breathing heavily and she had a feeling he was going to break off the embrace. But then he closed his eyes and wrapped his arms all the way around her until his forearms were on her back. He tilted her off center and kissed the holy heaven out of her.

His mouth was hard on hers. No more gentle searching, no soft caressing. A man's passion unleashed, a male's primal need given free rein. She absorbed him, welcoming the rush, the demand of him—

Spike's voice carried into the room. "Hey, Lex, where—whoa. Ah…sorry."

As she and Alex broke apart, Cass felt a rush of blood hit her face. The blush got worse as Spike quickly started backing out of the room and shutting the double doors.

"Wait up, buddy. I need a ride home," Alex said.

The man gave him a long look. Kind of like someone would if their friend was thinking of jumping off a bridge: *You crazy idiot.*

"Now?" Spike asked.

Alex stepped back. "Yeah."

"Do you have to go?" Cass whispered as the sound of oohs and aahs joined all the popping and cracking coming from outdoors.

"It's better if I do." He lifted his hand to her face and brushed her lips once with his thumb. Then he limped out of the room.

Chapter Twelve

As Spike pulled up to the workshop, Alex reached for the door handle. "Thanks, man. Eventually I'll be able to drive again."

"You know I'm cool with being your taxi." Spike looked across the seats. "Ah, listen, Lex, it's none of my business—"

"You're right."

"But I'm a nosy bastard."

"Just my luck."

"What's doing between you and Cass? I mean, she's righteous beautiful and a really good person, so I get all that. But if you want her and she wants you, why don't you just muscle O'Banyon out of the picture? He's a tank under all those pinstripes, but you could serve him up."

"You know it's more complicated than that."

When Spike fell silent, Alex glanced over.

The man's yellow eyes were narrow as he stared out of the front windshield. In the glow from the dashboard, his face was grim, his saw-toothed, jet-black hair like a cap of thorns on his head.

"You okay, Spike?"

"Brace yourself. I'm about to go sissy on you."

Alex had to smile. "Just as long as you don't try and hold my hand."

"Look, I know that what happened with your partner is eating you alive. And I think it's more than just about him being gone. Did you try and save him, Alex? Did you try and save him and lose him in the end?"

Alex recoiled.

"Yeah," Spike said softly. "That's it, isn't it. You lost him out on that boat, didn't you?"

"How do you…"

Spike's eyes flipped across the seat. They seemed to glimmer, becoming otherworldly in their golden intensity.

"We've all got demons, man. Some we work through. Some are ghosts we foxtrot into the grave with. But here's the thing. Time's short. Life's shorter. A blink of an eye and you've missed what you wanted, what you needed." Spike looked back out into the night. "Death's damn cold and it lasts forever once it shakes your hand. So take the warmth now, my man. Take it where you find it. Forgive yourself just enough to let some in, okay?"

Alex stared at his buddy and frowned. "What the hell happened to you?"

Spike's dark smile brought chills. "Ah, but we're talking about your curse, not mine. Now if you don't mind, I've got a party to get back to. There are a number of women dying to take advantage of my charms, and I'm in the mood to be used."

Alex got out of the car. Before he shut the door, he leaned down. "I just realized something. I don't know all that much about you. Where are you from, anyway?"

Spike moved the gearshift back and forth in Neutral. His sun-colored eyes flashed. "Oz."

Alex chuckled. "Which one are you? The lion, the scarecrow?"

Spike winked and put the car in gear. "The wizard."

Alex shut the door and watched the Honda take off down the drive, wondering what was in his friend's past.

Then he took a couple of deep breaths, sucking the cold night into his lungs.

Leaving Cassandra had been the right thing to do. It wasn't just that O'Banyon was up and the last thing she needed was to get caught between two jealous men. It was mostly because if he'd stayed much longer, he would have taken her back to the shop with him and woken up next to her in the morning. And he would have…finished.

Which was a bad idea, all the way around. Just because he'd outed his need for her, didn't mean the essential dynamic between them had changed.

So it was just as well that O'Banyon was with her over the weekend.

Well, provided Alex didn't think about the two of them together.

Cursing himself, he went into the shop and fired up the potbellied stove, stoking it for the night. He undressed and hit the mattress. As the temperature rose, he shoved the covers from his upper body and flopped onto his back.

Staring at the ceiling, he thought of Spike's words.

What if he could forgive himself a little? Just enough to have Cassandra once. Only once. The aftermath would be a tossing sea of guilt, but the taking…the taking would be wondrous.

God, he was a bastard, he thought. To even think such a thing.

He turned his head and looked at the desk where his father's plans were laid out.

His father never would have found himself in this situation. Ted Moorehouse had had honor. Honor in the life he'd led and in how he cared for the people who mattered.

Alex was ashamed to admit it, but he had pitied his father. Had been so focused on the brighter horizon he hadn't understood how someone could live such a small life.

Now he would settle for being half the man his father had been.

Alex closed his eyes and went back into the past. He saw barbecues on the front lawn with his father at the grill and him shucking corn on the back step. He remembered ice fishing on the lake in March when they'd shared hot chocolate and rubbed their hands over a little propane heater. He returned to the times he and his father had climbed the mountain behind the house in the spring and gotten mud in their boots.

Funny, he couldn't recall much about the last five finish lines he'd crossed. He'd gone past so many that the particulars of each one were a blur now.

The memories of his father, though, were as vivid as the experiences had been. He could bring up the smells of smoke and molasses off the grill, the taste of the cocoa, the mucky, creepy feeling of having mud slide around the inside of his boot like a molten sock.

And those things had happened twenty years ago.

God, he had lost so much, and the losing had started before his father and mother had died. It had started when he'd left his family behind.

Alex took a deep breath and tried to let go, but his regrets had set up shop and were staying put. They were like an ant farm in his chest, little paths of teeming remorse, always moving, always shifting, never, ever getting free.

He had to smile, thinking this was a hell of a way to break in the New Year. All around the world people were partying and blowing shooters and pitching confetti. Meanwhile, he was in bed with one hell of a dominatrix: Mistress Conscience.

Sometime later Alex came awake to the feel of something on his chest: a soft stroke over his naked skin.

He shot up and grabbed hold of—

"Cassandra? What are you doing here?" He released her wrist as he realized how very naked he was. He pulled the blankets up farther on his chest.

Oh, she was lovely. She had changed into casual clothes, and her hair was loose around her shoulders, a thick curtain of copper red.

When she knelt down by the side of the bed, he propped himself up on his arms.

"Is there something wrong?" he asked.

"Did you know?" she whispered into the darkness.

"Know what?"

There was a long pause. "That I wanted you. When Reese was alive. Was that why you didn't like me?"

Shocked, he studied her fine, delicate profile, lingering on her lips.

Good God…

"Did you?" he said roughly. "Did you want me?"

"I think so. I mean, there was that one moment. After you came out of the shower…"

Alex's heart went into a flat-out sprint.

Cassandra wrapped her arms around herself. "I just want you to know something. Whatever you sensed about me, or picked up on…I didn't realize it. I didn't even know until very recently." She looked at him. "I swear to you, I—"

"I never thought you were attracted to me."

"Oh." She stayed curled up tight, looking beyond him, at the wall.

"Cassandra, don't worry. I know you loved him. You have nothing to feel badly about."

Her shoulders eased a little. "Thank you. Thank you…for saying that. I took my wedding vows seriously and I never— I was always faithful to him."

They were quiet for a long time, the muffled crackle from the fire in the stove the only sound between them. He found looking at her down-turned face an absolute privilege. But she really needed to go.

Tonight, for whatever reason, the shield and sword of his guilt had been put down. And he felt as if there was nothing to keep him from her.

"Cassandra, is there something else?"

"Yes."

She moved so fast, she startled him. She lunged up and her lips found his, her hands diving into his hair, her tongue entering him in a slick rush.

Oh… She was so good.

He let her push him down onto the mattress as his mind spun.

She was going to take him. She had come to take him.

And…holy hell, he was going to let her. He was going to let her do anything she wanted to him.

Spike was right. Life was short, and warmth was fleeting, and the cold would last forever.

Just this once, he thought, giving up, giving in.

Only once. And then never again.

"Yes," he said, answering the question she wasn't asking, answering it for himself. "Yes…only tonight, but yes."

She pulled back and swept off the fleece she was wearing. Her breasts were bare, and in the glow from the potbellied stove, the sight of her had his hips surging up from the bed. She rose to her feet and stripped out of her jeans, her eyes luminescent and powerful.

With a single movement she swept the covers from his body and her eyes raked down him from head to foot. She looked at all of him, his skin, his muscles, his bones, his scars.

His wild physical response to her.

Then she lay on top of him, her silken body covering him, her thigh sinking between his, her belly absorbing the thick length of his arousal.

I love you, he thought, rubbing himself against her, sinking into her and getting lost. She was all of his fantasies and more. Flesh and blood bringing what he had dreamed of to life.

"You're so beautiful," he groaned.

He bent up and captured her mouth, reveling in the sensation of their lips and tongues meeting. Her body shifted to the side and slid off his. He turned instinctually toward her, but her hand stopped him.

"I want to touch you," she said, kissing his neck.

And she did. Everywhere. When she reached the place where he ached the most, the shock of the contact was enough to take him to the brink. He steadied her hand, stopping her from stroking him.

"I'm about to— That is, I don't want to…not unless we're—"

Oh, yeah. He was smooth. Real smooth.

Funny, with other women, he'd had no trouble spelling out what he wanted and what the limits were. With Cassandra, he felt like a fourteen-year-old boy. All pounding hormones and raw vulnerability.

Then it happened.

Her smile as she held on to his flesh was so sexual, so womanly, so beautiful, it didn't matter she wasn't moving her hand anymore. His body surged, his lower back and thighs grabbing tight. The release shot out of him.

As the pleasure hit, horror curdled his blood. And would have sucked the testosterone right out of him if he hadn't lost it all a second and a half ago.

Damn it. He'd been a good lover once. Truly. At an earlier point in his life, he'd been rock-solid confident about his ability to pleasure a woman. But he couldn't catch a break with her. First time he'd had to stop. This time…

Alex squeezed his eyes shut and crossed his arms over his face as she let go of him.

Cass wanted to laugh, and not with cruelty or out of awkward disappointment. The truth was, she was thrilled that Alex had lost control.

In all her life, she'd never been a seducer. Had never had the kind of confidence it took to ravish a man. But tonight, with Alex, she felt…different.

"I'm sorry about that," he said gruffly. His voice was muffled beneath his forearms.

She wasn't. His lapse made her feel erotic and powerful. Especially because discipline was so much a part of him. The idea that she'd burrowed beneath that strength was…well, it changed a little bit of how she saw herself.

"It's okay, these things happen—" She stopped as he winced.

Yeah, that probably wasn't what he wanted to hear right now.

As the silence stretched out, she thought she probably should go. She kissed him on the chest and sat up, swinging her legs over the side of the bed. The floor was chilly on the soles of her feet.

"Well…" she murmured. "I guess I'll see you—"

It happened so fast that her head spun. Literally.

One minute she was on the verge of standing up. The next, she was flat on her back with Alex on top of her.

He smoothed her hair from her face as he parted her legs with his knee. His hips moved against her and…wow, okay. Recovery time was over.

"You understand that I can't have you leaving just yet."

"Male pride?" she said with a smile.

"The need to be with you." He nuzzled her neck. "And, yeah, okay, a little male pride."

She arched as he found the tip of her breast with his fingers and he pulled away, looking down at her as he lightly brushed her nipple. She moaned at the sensation, throwing her head back.

His voice was low. "Do you have any idea how beautiful you are?"

Well, when he looked at her like that, she had a pretty clear idea.

His hands were slow and thorough as they explored her

body, leaving a path of heat in their wake. She was shaking with need when he reached between her legs.

"Oh, Cassandra," he said as he touched her heat.

She cried out and bit into his shoulder.

The mattress wiggled as he kissed a path down her body. But then he stopped and cursed.

"This bed is too damn small. I feel like I'm making love to you in a shoe box." He tried to reposition himself, shifting this way and that, but his arms and legs and torso wouldn't fit no matter how much he tried.

With a growl of frustration, he came back up and covered her with his weight. "Now. Cassandra, I want you now."

"Yes…"

His tongue shot into her mouth as his hand came between them. She felt blunt warmth brushing against her and then his thick arousal slid into her body. He shuddered as they were joined, and she felt the shaking inside of her.

"Is this okay?" he asked tightly.

"Please…more…"

With his first powerful thrust, she knew there would be no stopping. His rhythm was strong, dominating, his heavy, muscular body churning above her. The surging took her right to heaven, her release shooting through her in waves, stiffening her, stealing the air from her lungs, the sight from her eyes, the sound from her ears.

Alex paused, as if savoring the way her body grabbed on to his, and then as soon as she stilled, he took over again. He held nothing back, spared her no ounce of his weight and strength and need as he drove his hips over and over again. She held on to him at the waist, her arms sliding up and down the small of his back as he pumped, his skin blooming with sweat.

Tension built within his body as his driving hips went faster and faster, the stroke of his retreats getting shorter and shorter.

And then in a mighty yell, he called out her name and pushed inside one last time. The force of his release took her over the edge with him.

As they held on to each other, tears blinded her eyes.

So very good. So very…perfect.

As dawn arrived, Alex stared at Cassandra while she slept.

He'd watched her since the moment he'd rolled off her after they'd made love. Which had been hours ago.

The idea of closing his eyes and missing even a moment of having her beside him in his bed was unthinkable.

She was curled up against his body, seeking his warmth to fend off the chill of the shop. The potbellied stove had burned through its supply of wood, but there was no way he was getting up and re-stoking it. He was hoping if he didn't disturb her, she would sleep until noontime. Tomorrow.

He wondered what her mood was going to be when she woke up. Would she regret what they'd done in the night? Even if she didn't, she was probably going to be sore. He'd never been like that with anyone, never unleashed his body with such total abandon.

Then again, he'd never wanted someone so desperately.

Cassandra stirred and nestled deeper into his shoulder. Her brows met as if she were confused. Her eyes opened.

Alex braced himself for her reaction.

She looked up at him. And smiled.

I love you, he thought, his body heating up.

"Hi," he said. Like an idiot.

"Hi." Her voice was husky. She glanced at the potbellied stove. "It's a little cold."

Leaving her was the last thing he wanted to do, but he rolled off the bed and went naked to the woodpile. When he had the fire going, he pulled on a pair of jeans, tucking himself in so his need wasn't so obvious.

He hated that morning had come and their time together was over.

"Are you all right?" he asked, turning toward her.

"Yes."

"I don't regret last night," he blurted.

Her gaze dropped to the floor and she pulled the blankets up.

"Are you sure about that?" she said tightly.

He frowned and then heard his own words. *I don't regret last night.*

Oh, yeah, that was exactly what a woman wanted to hear from a man she'd been with.

He went to the bed and lowered himself to his knees on the floor beside her. He opened his mouth. Words failed him, which was not a surprise. The ones he really wanted to say he needed to keep to himself.

Cassandra held the blankets to her chest as she sat up and swung her feet off the bed. "I should go."

"Wait…" He reached out and touched her face with both hands. "Oh…beautiful woman."

He pressed himself between her legs, sweeping his fingers through her hair.

"Just once more," he said, kissing her neck. He searched his mind, begging it to come up with the right way to speak to her. He'd been rat awful about so many things and not just this morning. "I…want to make love with you. Just one more time. Before you go."

He pressed his lips to her collarbone. Her shoulder.

"Will you let me?" he whispered as he moved his head back and forth, his lips brushing over her skin.

She said nothing. But she let the blankets drop from her body.

Chapter Thirteen

Days later Cassandra stood in the White Caps kitchen and stared at the clipboard she was holding. What was she… Right, she was making a note about the main drainage line.

Except, as her pen hit the page, her mind came up with a big fat zero.

What was…?

Ted cleared his throat.

"Um, boss? You were saying?" When she looked at him blankly, he murmured, "About the upstairs hallway?"

"Oh, yes. Sorry. It would be great if you guys could lay down the plywood in preparation for the flooring installation."

The man's gaze shifted over her shoulder and widened. She turned around.

Spike was coming through the kitchen doorway, and immediately she searched for Alex behind him.

The plastic flap just settled back into place, however.

It had been three days since she'd left the shop in the early morning, three days since she'd last seen Alex. He hadn't gone to any of the other parties at Joy and Gray's over the weekend, not the festivities on Saturday night or the brunch on Sunday.

She knew he was avoiding her.

He had said only one night. Evidently, he'd meant it.

As Spike came up to her, she returned his hip check and forced herself to smile. "Hey, there, big guy."

He grinned. "You gonna show me around your playground?"

"Sure. Ted, are we finished?"

Ted was too busy staring at Spike's pierced ears and hair and tattoos to answer.

Spike looked back at the man. Then brought his hands up quick and made star bursts out of them. "Boo!"

Ted actually did a jump and shuffle before backing to the door. "Um...I'll see you tomorrow, boss."

Cass waited until the plastic flap fell into place. "Did you have to do that?"

"Come on, the guy needed the exercise."

She rolled her eyes. "Not really."

As they walked through the house, she pointed out all the progress.

When they were upstairs, she paused in one of the bathrooms. "Plumber starts tomorrow. Electrician, too."

"You're doing great work."

"It's all of us. I've got a good crew."

"Yeah, even though they scare easy."

The two of them returned to the kitchen and she packed up her things, putting her cell phone and her clipboard in her knapsack along with the sandwich she should have eaten for lunch.

"So, Cass, I've got a favor to ask."

"Name it."

He held the plastic sheet back so she could step through it. Outside, the cold was sharp enough to filet her parka.

Boy, the Adirondacks did frigid well. The place was one giant icebox this time of year.

"I was wondering if you'd take Alex into town tonight. I've got something I need to take care of so I can't do the chauffeuring thing."

She hesitated. "Does he know that you're asking me this?"

"Oh, sure. Absolutely."

"Where's he going?"

"Here and there. He's ready now." Spike went over to the Honda. "Thanks, Cass."

As the man tore out of the driveway, she looked to the shop.

There was no reason to be immature about this, she told herself. They'd been together a couple of times. That was it. Sure, their history was complicated, but if he could be cool about what had happened, so could she.

She walked up the snow-covered lawn and knocked on the door.

Alex called out, "Come in! I'm almost good to go."

See, his voice was casual. Calm. He was fine. She was fine. They were both fine.

Cass walked in. Alex was at the desk, his big body curled over a set of sailboat plans. Pencil shavings and eraser debris covered the blue paper he was working on.

"Hey, man, you eat yet?" Alex said without looking up. "We can suck back a plate or two at the Silver Diner when we're through. Maybe rack some balls at Greene's. What do you say?"

"I think Spike is a liar."

Alex's head shot up. "Cassandra."

She lifted her hand and then thought, why was she waving at him? "I'm, er, I'm supposed to be your ride tonight. Wherever you're going. Spike asked me to fill in for him."

Alex muttered something under his breath. "Look, let me call Libby. You don't have to do this."

"It's all right."

"You've worked hard all day—"

"If you don't want to go with me, just say so, okay?" Her words cracked through the room like a whip.

Alex stood up and reached for his cane. "I was trying to be polite."

"Sorry," she muttered. As her eyes flipped to the bed, she had to turn away from it.

Fine my fat fanny, she thought. Her head was a total mess.

The thing was, she'd assumed he'd seek her out even though he'd said their night together was a one-time-only kind of thing. It was just…he'd wanted to be with her so badly. And the way he'd made love to her in the morning light…

But she should have known better. Alex Moorehouse was all about discipline. What he said, he meant. Clearly his feelings for his Miracle were more important than his body's needs.

Alex limped over to her. "Actually, I'd much rather have you behind the wheel. Spike swears at the other cars, he never uses his directional signal and he can't parallel park worth a damn. I'm not even sure he has a license."

Cass glanced up at his face and wished she felt as relaxed as he looked. "Where are we going?"

"To see my grandmother. She's in a nursing home now. Joy used to take care of her, but the dementia has gotten to the point that professional supervision is required. And it's important for Joy to have a life." He went over to a leather jacket that was hanging on the wall. "I make sure I go see her a couple times a week. I'm the only one she recognizes, although that's because she thinks I'm her father. So I guess that doesn't count, does it?"

He pulled the coat on and held the door open.

"Would you mind if I used your ladies' room first?" Cass asked.

"Sure." He closed out the cold. "Take your time."

When she came back, he was putting his cell phone up to his ear.

"Moorehouse." There was a pause and then, "Mad Dog! What the hell? How did you— He did? Figures. Nah, I'm glad it's you." There was a long silence. Then his face darkened. "I don't know. I'm working on it. Good. Better. You're what? Mad Dog— No... For God's sake, I don't— Damn it." His lips thinned. "Yes, I'll be here. Now, tell me the truth. In an earlier life, you were Genghis Khan, right?" He laughed, and his voice dropped, warmth coming through it. "I'll see you soon, Mad. I've missed you."

When he ended the call, he glanced over. "You ready?"

Cass nodded.

As they went out to the Rover, he said, "That was a member of my crew."

"Oh?"

"Yeah. Mad Dog is...extraordinary. One of a kind."

"You sound as if you really respect him." She opened the driver's side door.

"Her. Madeline is a her."

Cass looked over the SUV's hood. As Alex got into the car, he was wearing a little half smile the likes of which she had never seen before.

After Cassandra parked the car, Alex eased himself out of the Range Rover and made sure his balance was steady before he started walking. The snow was packed solid, which meant there was a gloss on the top that was slicker than baby oil.

"Need help?" Cassandra asked brusquely, as if she knew he'd only turn her down.

He looked over at her. In the waning sunlight, her hair gleamed like copper flashing and the cold wind had coaxed a blush out of her cheeks. She looked tired, though, the shadows under her eyes suggesting she hadn't slept well lately.

He knew all about insomnia, too.

The last three days had been hell. He'd wanted to see her again the instant she'd left the shop that morning. But a vow was a vow and he'd already technically broken the once-only rule by being with her after she'd woken up.

Unable to trust himself around her, he'd skipped the rest of the parties that weekend. Besides, God only knew what O'Banyon had had to say when she'd disappeared all night long. There was no reason to get brawling with the guy.

Besides, only once was all he would allow himself. He owed Reese's memory, for one thing. But more significant, he was very sure that if Cassandra knew he'd killed her husband she wouldn't want him anymore. Since he wasn't about to tell her the truth, because that would just add another layer to her tragedy, then he had no right to be with her again.

"Alex?" She tilted her head, green eyes widening.

Shoot, he'd been staring at her.

"Sorry." He smiled. "After you."

Evergreen Assisted Living was housed in a single-story brick building that, unfortunately, looked a lot like a prison from the outside. The facility was all dull gray concrete, uniform windows, and doors with alarms on them. As he and Cassandra walked inside, however, the place's true nature came alive. There were bright murals and real plants. A cage full of pink and blue and yellow parakeets. From the rec room, big band-era music drifted out.

One of the aides bustled by with a tray of cookies and stopped when she saw him. "Hello, Alex! Our Emma's been waiting for you all day long."

"Hi, Marlene. Hey, how's your grandson?"

The woman flushed and cleared her throat. "Aren't you sweet to ask. He's much better since he got to meet you. All he talks about now is sailing."

"You tell him I always got a place on my crew for a good man."

Marlene reached out her hand, touching his arm. She blinked rapidly a couple of times. "Thank you. Really...thank you."

The gratitude made him uncomfortable and Marlene seemed to know it. She smiled and patted him before stepping back.

"Listen, you don't really have to come to his birthday party," she said.

"Are you nuts? And miss the cake? Besides, he's asked me to check out a girl for him. You know, see if she's got what it takes. Gotta have my boy's back. It's a guy thing."

Marlene looked as if she was about to melt again and

he was relieved when she just put her hand to her throat, nodded and left.

It wasn't that he minded tears. He'd always felt, though, that if a woman cried in front of him, he had to fix whatever it was that had upset her. And some things, like what had happened to Marlene's grandson, just couldn't be made right. At least not in the ways that mattered, not in the ways that would ensure the kid grew up and lived a full life and passed gently into the grave at the age of ninety.

Frankly the gratitude was weird, as if he were doing her a favor. Like he would turn down a request from a child in a burn unit? Whose company he enjoyed?

"We're down here," he said to Cassandra, nodding toward a corridor that stretched out to the right.

Every twenty feet there was a door, and some of them were open. Inside, residents watched TV from loungers or lay in bed reading or sleeping. Some of them looked up and the ones who did waved. He returned the greetings.

"Yo, martini!" he called out to one gentleman.

"Hiya, gin fizz!" the guy shouted back.

Alex paused in front of his grandmother's closed door. He made sure his shirt was tucked in smoothly. Adjusted his belt so the buckle was precisely in the middle. Ran his hands through his hair, noting that it had to be cut.

He took a deep breath. As he wrapped his fingers around the handle, he glanced at Cassandra.

She was staring at him with an odd expression on her face.

"What?" He looked down at himself. "What's wrong?"

"Nothing. I—you just surprise me, that's all."

"Why?"

"You seem very human tucking in your shirt and smoothing your hair. That's all."

"Human?" God, had having sex with him convinced her he was some kind of animal?

The door was torn out of his hand before he could say anything else. The aide on the other side, a young woman with a blond ponytail, jumped.

"Oh! Hello!" She went breathless as she looked up at him and blushed the color of a Christmas ribbon.

"Hi, Lizzie."

"Hi— I mean—" She bumped into the doorjamb as she came out, her blue eyes fixated on his face. "Hi. Um, she's asleep."

"Okay. I'll just hang for a minute or two and leave her a note. I shouldn't have come this late."

"Do you want me to help you wake her up?"

"Nah. Leave her be." Alex motioned Cassandra inside with his arm.

"Will you be back tomorrow?" Lizzie asked, bringing her ponytail around her shoulder and petting it. "Because she likes to have her hair done for when you come. She and I have such fun when I put it up for her. She just loves that. And she loves seeing you."

"I'll come the day after. And thanks for taking such good care of her."

"I like her. A lot."

Alex waved as the door eased shut. Hero worship coupled with a tender crush was as hard for him to handle as gratitude. In his mind, both magnified his faults to an unbearable clarity.

His grandmother's room was dim, lit only by a night light glowing in the bathroom. The furnishings were institutional, like something you'd find in a college dorm, and the air smelled a little of disinfectant, but other than that, it was a very nice place. Lots of windows. Bright yellow walls. Everything was clean.

There were family pictures on every flat space in the room: the windowsill, the bureau, the bookcase by the door, the walls. A bouquet of fresh flowers, probably brought by Joy before she returned to New York City, was on a side table.

"Hello, grandmother," Alex murmured as he approached the bed.

Emma Moorehouse had always been beautiful, and in her gentle slumber, she was still lovely at age eighty-eight. Her wavy, white hair flowed around her, spilling onto the Frette pillowcase and her peach satin duvet. Her face was unlined and pale as cream, the result of careful tending, not plastic surgery: she'd always taken a parasol outside with her, and that classic, high-bred bone structure had withstood the passage of the decades with grace.

He carefully picked up her hand. The skin on the back of it was translucent, so thin he could practically see the bones.

"It's Lexi, Grandmother," he said softly, while he smoothed her fingers.

She stirred and turned toward his voice, though her eyes remained closed.

"I've brought someone with me. Cassandra. She's working on our house."

Alex talked for a while, saying nothing much. For some reason, being around her eased him and the feeling was evidently mutual. When the dementia got bad, even with the drugs Emma was on, the nursing home would call him and he'd come running. All it took was the sound of his voice and she'd calm down.

It was odd to be the source of comfort for someone. But over the past month or so, he'd grown to need the sensation he got from being needed by her.

Cass settled back against the wall and fought the urge to give Alex privacy. She just didn't want to leave. Seeing such kindness in him relieved the tension in her somehow, even though his compassion was directed toward another.

As Alex loomed over the bed in that black leather jacket, he didn't seem at all the kind of person who could be so gentle. But this massive, hard man had tremendous reserves of tenderness. He just kept them to himself a lot of the time.

And he was wrong about being awkward around people. Everyone at the facility adored him. The staff, the patients.

How could they not? He cut a stunning figure to begin with. Add to the looks his innate charisma and his calm confidence and he was the leader no matter what space he walked through or who was in it. She was quite certain he could rally everyone in the nursing home with a mere passing suggestion.

"I'm working on some of Dad's plans," she heard him say. And then, "Do you think he would have minded?"

In the low light, Alex's face was mostly somber, but in his expression she caught a glimpse of something so sweet her heart cracked: a hint of the little boy he had once been.

An awful feeling came over her, something tantamount to dread.

No, it actually *was* dread.

She couldn't possibly be falling in love with him. No way.

No. This was not happening.

Cass closed her eyes and let her head fall back. When

it hit something, she turned around. The framed photograph was of a young man who looked like Alex.

"My father," Alex said softly into her ear.

Cass jumped and glanced over her shoulder. "Ah, you two look alike."

He reached out and squared off the picture. His blunt fingers lingered on the frame.

"I'm sorry," she said, abruptly.

He frowned, but didn't look away from the photograph. "Why?"

"For the loss of your parents. Gray told me how they died. It must have been very difficult for you. All of you."

She expected him to shrug her off. Instead he murmured, "If Reese could come back, would you do anything different?"

Cass hesitated, the question catching her off guard. "Yes. Yes, I would."

"What would it be?"

Oh, God, she thought. So much.

"I, uh, I would have let him know what I was thinking more often." Even though it would have hastened the disintegration of their marriage. If the infidelity had been out in the open between them, she knew in her heart she couldn't have stayed, and it was disturbing to realize that the subterfuge had been what kept her with Reese. Why lies were more binding than the truth just didn't make sense.

Didn't sit well with her, either.

Alex nodded. "Me, too. I would have told my father how much he meant to me. And I would have spent more time with him. My mother as well. Anyway… Let's go, okay?"

On their way out of the nursing home, they stopped so Alex could chat with the rehab specialist about his grandmother.

When they were in the Rover, Cass looked over at him. "You are so good with her."

Alex's face tightened as he put his seat belt on. "It's weird. We weren't close when I was growing up. I thought of her as rigid and old-fashioned, but now I love her for those very things. The high standards of behavior. The Victorian code she lived by. When she dies, it's going to devastate me."

Cass stayed quiet, hoping he'd forget he was talking with such candor.

Fortunately, he kept going.

"Because of this leg of mine…I've had a chance to get to know her again." He shook his head. "God, if I hadn't been forced to come home, I wouldn't have. Maybe not even for Frankie's or Joy's weddings. And how whacked is that?"

"Racing is a very demanding profession. I'm sure they would have understood."

He looked at her. "But why should they have to? You know, I didn't realize how much slack the family cut me until recently. When I came back after the accident, all banged up, my sisters welcomed me with open arms, as if I hadn't run off and left them when they needed me." He swore softly. "Success doesn't put you in a special class, it really doesn't. It just predisposes you to behaving badly. Or at least that's what it's done to me. Frankie raised Joy. Joy took care of Grand-Em. The two of them sacrificed their lives while I chased after finish lines. The only solace that I take is they both ended up with men worthy enough to love them and strong enough to take care of them. But still…it's a damn shame I can't replay the past. And I really wish there was some way to make up for the great void that is their brother."

Alex frowned, as if he'd just realized how much he'd said.

Before she could get a word in, he said smoothly, "Do you mind if we stop at the supermarket on the way home?"

His sudden shift jarred her. One minute he was telling her things she'd never imagined hearing from him. The next, he was back to stone-cold normal.

"Cassandra?"

"Uh, no problem."

"Thanks."

Man, this guy could close doors better than anyone she'd ever met, Cass thought as she put the car in gear. In an earlier life, he'd no doubt been a brass hinge.

When they were going down the Lake Road, he withdrew a thick envelope from his pocket. "Can we pull up to that mailbox by the stoplight?"

"Sure." She eased over to the curb and eyed the snowbank. "Let me drop it in for you."

He hesitated and then gave the thing to her. "Thanks."

When she was at the box, she glanced down at the address he'd written in precise letters. Newport, Rhode Island. She didn't recognize the name.

The trip to the local Shop Rite didn't take long in spite of how much he bought. Alex was efficient. He knew exactly what he wanted and where to find it in the aisles. Six packs of Ensure. PowerBars. Chicken. Chicken. Chicken. Lettuce heads. Carrots. Vitamins. Orange juice. Yogurt. He worked the U-Scan like a flash, as well.

The bags were in the back and they were heading to White Caps, when Alex looked over at her.

"Thanks for doing this. I'm sure there are better ways for you to blow an hour and a half."

"It was no problem." She hit the turn signal and eased

onto his driveway. "Would you like some help getting this stuff inside?"

"No. You wait here with the heater running. I won't take long."

And he didn't, even with the cane.

With the last two bags in his left hand, he shut the rear door. She expected him just to wave her off, but he came around to the driver's side. She put the window down.

"Seriously, thank you," he said.

Their eyes met.

Ask me in, she thought. Ask me to stay for a while. For the night. I know you have your reasons to keep away, but—

"See you tomorrow, Cassandra."

Chapter Fourteen

A week later Alex clipped his cell phone shut and stared at the thing.

William Hosworth IV, or Hoss as he was known in sailing circles, wanted to buy a boat. From Alex.

Which was nuts, he thought.

When he'd sent those plans to Rhode Island, he hadn't anticipated this kind of thing. He'd just wanted another set of eyes to tell him if the changes he'd made to his father's designs had in fact improved the overall performance of the craft.

What the hell did he know about building a sailboat? Sure, he'd spent hours upon hours rehabbing the damn things in and out of the water. And there wasn't anything he couldn't do with his hands.

But building a sailboat from start to finish was a different beast than fixing one.

Abruptly he thought of the unwinterized part of the barn. If it was cleared out, the center aisle was big enough to accommodate a full-size yacht up on blocks. If he bought the wood and hired a couple of guys—

No way. He'd need industrial tools and respiratory apparatuses. He'd have to comply with standards and codes he didn't know about.

Except, what if he out-sourced the project? Now there was an idea. He knew a pair of brothers up on Blue Mountain Lake who handmade repros of old-fashioned power boat racers. Maybe they'd be interested in doing a partnership.

Then Alex thought of Mad Dog's impending visit. He knew it wasn't a social one. His crew was going to want him back at the helm. Soon.

If he decided to return as their captain, he could kiss off the yacht-building fantasy. You didn't put boats together as a hobby even if you had someone else pounding the nails. You had to monitor the progress constantly, be on hand and available if problems arose.

Like Cassandra was with her work. She was on site every day, dealing with issues.

He looked at White Caps, hoping to catch a glimpse of her. Instead all he saw were three plumbers walking out with their toolboxes.

Each afternoon when the men left, Alex fought not to go over to the house. Cassandra's presence was a constant—

A pounding on the door brought his head around.

"Hey, Moorehouse!" Spike called out. "You ready to go see your grandmother?"

"Yeah." He picked up two of his father's original plans and tucked them under his arm as Spike came in. "And I've got another stop I need to make in town."

"No problem, man." Spike smiled, his typical, half-cocked grin making an appearance.

Today, the guy was wearing his standard uniform. Black turtleneck, black pants, beat-to-hell biker's jacket. A pair of aviator sunglasses hung on a leash around his neck. With his hair sticking straight up and the earrings, he looked like a *GQ* model who'd been styled by a goth anarchist.

Alex grabbed his coat and the two of them went outside. Snow was falling lightly, silently. He looked to White Caps, willing Cassandra to come out. Of course, she didn't.

"Why don't you go to her, man?" Spike said quietly.

Alex just shook his head and got in the car.

After the plumbers left, Cass sagged against the wall. She felt as if the law of gravity was taking a special interest in her. Her clothes seemed heavy as a lead suit, her arms and legs dragging.

It was all catching up to her. The not sleeping, the not eating.

Bottom line? She was losing weight as well as her mind.

And all that was before she'd realized she had fallen in love with Alex.

The sound of a car pulling up to the house brought her head around. Actually, the low growl was more like a diesel truck. So it was probably one of the plumbers coming back for something he'd forgotten.

As the plastic wrap moved aside, Cass had to blink several times.

Holy…that was definitely *not* one of the plumbers.

The woman in the doorway was easily six feet tall, and her face was right out of the movies, all eyes and lips. She was dressed in tight blue jeans and a dark fleece and her long, black hair fell down her back.

She glowed with good health, positively radiated strength and vitality. Next to her Cass felt like a shrub with frost burn.

"Hi, I'm looking for Alex Moorehouse. He said he lived here." The woman looked around with sapphire eyes. "But I must have the wrong address."

"He, ah, he lives in the shop."

"You mean the barn? Oh, great. Thanks." The woman turned away.

"Who are you?" Cass asked quietly.

"Madeline Maguire. I'm his navigator." She flashed a smile. Naturally, her teeth were perfect and as white as tile.

"Mad Dog."

The woman laughed, a deep, husky sound. "You must be a friend of his."

"Not really. No."

Mad Dog gave her an odd look. "Well, anyway. Thanks for the redirection."

Cass went to one of the few windows that had some glass left in it and watched the woman jog up to the shop, her body moving with the power and agility of a superior athlete.

Just like Alex's did.

Cass collected her things and shut off the generator. She was about to leave when the plastic flap was thrown to the side again.

Madeline smiled, warmth and apology combined. "If he's not there, you wouldn't happen to know where he might have gone?"

"I'm sorry, I don't." But then she remembered seeing Spike arrive and leave about an hour ago. "Wait. He probably went into town. He shouldn't be long."

At that moment the Honda came down the drive and pulled up to the shop.

"Here he is."

The woman glanced over her shoulder. "I wonder how this is going to go," she said softly.

"Excuse me?"

"It's been a while and a lot has happened," Madeline murmured. "God, look at him move. So carefully."

Alex eased out of the car and leaned on his cane while he waved Spike off. Before he started for the shop, he eyed the black Dodge Viper the woman had evidently come in.

"Mad Dog!" he called toward the shop. "Where are you?"

Mad Dog, Madeline, whatever her name was, burst out of the plastic and jogged with that awful grace across the lawn.

Cass followed, going to her car.

"I'm right here," the woman said.

Alex looked over his shoulder. The woman stopped about ten yards away from him.

"Hey, girl," he said, as he turned around.

"Captain."

He smiled slowly. "So you gonna hug me or just keep staring at me like you've seen a ghost?"

The woman let out a soft sob and galloped into his arms.

As their bodies melded, Cass closed her eyes.

Fumbling for her keys, she got in the Rover and drove to Gray's. When she was parked in front of the house, she put her head down on the steering wheel. The car was freezing cold by the time she went inside.

She gave Ernest a brief hello and skirted the issue of dinner by telling Libby she'd eaten a big lunch with the workmen.

"And this might sound antisocial," she continued, "but I really want to lie down. Even though it's only six o'clock."

"You head on up to bed, then," Libby said. "You look exhausted. Oh, by the way, we're having visitors again. Alex's sister Frankie has asked everyone to come up here. Well, everyone being Joy and Gray, that is."

Cass frowned. "I hope she's not worried about the progress we're making at White Caps. I talk to her at least once a week to update her."

"I'm sure she's perfectly happy. Now get on up to bed, will you? You make me tired just looking at you. And if you wake up hungry at midnight, there's plenty in the fridge to snack on."

Upstairs, Cass took a quick shower and climbed between the sheets.

So why aren't you with your Miracle?

It can't work between us.

She's not in your life?

Not the way I wish she was. Not the way…I want her. It would be inappropriate.

Of course it would. Alex couldn't have a personal relationship with one of his crew, his navigator. And if the woman was indeed one of the strongest assets on his boat, he wasn't going to let her talents go to someone else. Clearly, he'd rather forgo the relationship for the winning. Which made him the professional, the champion, he was.

Madeline Maguire was his Miracle.

God, this hurts, Cass thought, massaging her chest. This really hurts.

Later that night Alex lay back against his pillow and glared at the ceiling. "I don't want you on my floor."

"Your leg trumps chivalry, Captain."

He rolled over onto his side and looked at Mad's face.

She was staring up at him, waiting for him to let her say the things she'd come to say. Over dinner in town and through several great racks of pool, they'd talked about the old times, the good times, and she'd caught him up on the crew's latest and greatest.

But that was all preamble. And they both knew it.

"So let's get it over with," he said.

"We want you back."

Alex almost smiled. The stories they'd shared over the Silver Diner's blue-plate special and then across all that green felt had gotten him thinking. Missing. Wishing.

The words just came out. "I want to come back."

"Thank God," Mad breathed.

"But I don't know when." He wasn't about to tell her that the state of his mind made his leg look like a real winner, so he focused on the physical stuff. "I've got a lot of rehab I need to do before I'm up and rolling. You'll see tomorrow, if you work out with us."

"Us?"

"Yeah. Me and Spike. You'll like him."

"I already like his name."

Alex chuckled. They were silent awhile, and then Mad murmured, "Captain?"

"Huh?"

"There's one more thing."

"Let it fly, Mad."

"The boys and me…we liked Reese. We were grateful for what he did for us. You know, all that money and support and he was a nice guy, too. His death, it shook us up. But we want you to know, if it had been you who hadn't come back, we, uh, we would have been ruined. We would have bailed on the sport. We wouldn't have been able to go on without you."

"Thanks, but you'd have gotten over it. Trust me." He thought of the deaths of his father and mother. He'd gone on. Gone on and left his sisters to clean up the mess, sure, but he'd moved ahead. God, he hated himself sometimes. He really did. "Now, enough of the sentimental stuff, okay?"

She laughed softly. "Aye, Captain."

They were silent for a time.

"Hey, Mad? I want you to be aware of something."

"What?"

"Reese's wife is working on White Caps. She's our architect and general contractor. I just wanted you to know in case you ran into her."

"The redhead? That was her?"

He tried to remember if Cassandra had come to any of the races and realized she hadn't. The only times he'd seen her were when he and Reese were going out on, or coming home from, private trips.

"You haven't met her, have you?" he said.

Mad shook her head. "You know how Reese was all into keeping his lives separate. I did see her from a distance at the funeral, but she looked so different then. I didn't recognize her today."

"She's been through a lot. Be…careful with her, okay?"

"Yeah, of course." Mad rolled over onto her back. "Funny, though."

"What?"

"When I asked if she was a friend of yours, she said she wasn't."

Alex cleared his throat. "Well, I suppose she isn't."

No, they were not friends and they never would be. They were not really lovers, either.

Cass's voice shot through his head, her words spoken during one of the arguments they'd had.

...after I leave this job, I'm never going to see you again...

Alex frowned as it dawned on him that the renovations on White Caps would be done in a month or two. Then she would go back to New York. And he would go back to the sea.

There would be no reason for their paths to cross again. Ever.

"You okay, Captain?" Mad said abruptly.

"What?"

"I heard a groan."

"Yeah, I'm fine, Mad. Go to sleep. Spike's showing up first thing for some serious ironmania."

"Aye, Captain."

Alex turned onto his back.

Death wasn't the only black hole someone could fall into, he thought. Divergent lives could do a damn good erase job, too.

A person could be perfectly healthy and above ground, and you could still lose them forever.

Chapter Fifteen

The next morning Alex stared out the picture window at White Caps and tried to imagine where Cassandra might be in the house.

X-ray powers would be really handy right about now, he thought.

Behind him, in the bathroom, Mad Dog was getting dressed to exercise and she was humming. Off-key. A truly horrible rendition of the theme from *Stars Wars*.

There was a pounding on the shop's door.

"Rock and roll," Alex said over his shoulder.

"You ready to work?" Spike called out as he walked in.

Alex nodded and took off his sweatshirt. "Yeah."

"Hey, that Viper is *sweet*. Whose is it?"

The bathroom door opened and Mad stepped out in a black sports bra and a pair of black panties.

"It's mine. Hi, I'm Madeline. You can call me Mad."

Alex had to swallow to keep from laughing. Spike looked like someone who'd been hit in the back of the head with a mast. The expression of awe and disbelief sank even deeper into his face as Mad sauntered right up to him, stuck her hand out and smiled.

As she stood in front of his buddy, Alex considered his navigator as a woman. Which was exactly what Spike was doing.

Yeah, Mad did have the whole Amazon-goddess thing working for her. She was tanned and muscled, but you definitely knew she was a female. And not just because her black hair was almost down to the small of her back.

He glanced at Spike. The guy was extending his hand slowly, like Mad was either an apparition or something that might take his arm off.

"Your hair is great," she said, taking his palm and giving it a good shake. "And I seriously dig the tat on your neck. How many do you have?"

Spike blinked. "A couple."

"Can I see them?"

Those yellow eyes actually popped. "Ah, not all of them, no."

"How about only the decent ones? I've never had the courage to get inked, but I love to look at them."

There was a pause.

"You mean now?" Spike asked.

Mad nodded and focused on his chest. Like she was looking forward to getting a load of it.

Spike glanced across the room at Alex and flared his eyelids a little, flashing the international masculine symbol for: Save my ass, buddy. Right now.

Alex nodded gravely and said, "Yeah, let's see 'em, Spike. Even the naughty ones."

Those yellow eyes spit such fire that Alex figured he had to relent. Either that or he was never getting a ride anywhere ever again.

"Okay, Mad, we better lay off."

Mad shrugged and headed for the weights. "Pity. So who's first with the iron?"

"Aren't you going to get dressed?" Spike muttered, pointedly looking anywhere else but her backside.

Mad cocked an eyebrow and looked down at herself. "I am dressed. I mean, I didn't bring my workout gear and this is just like a bikini."

Alex frowned, finding it hard to imagine she was missing the effect she had on Spike. The guy was actually sheepish, he was so blown away by her.

Who knew the guy even *had* sheepish in him?

Alex thought about her on those boats with all his men. She treated them the same way. Up front, on the level, with never a hint of anything sexual. Of course, that was a professional environment.

Had she ever been with anyone? Not that he knew of. And sailing was a very closed club with a gossip mill like a sorority house.

"Mad, toss on some shorts, will you? Before you burn Spike's retinas."

"Shorts? Who brings shorts to the Adirondacks in January? I almost took a dogsled to get here. And before you suggest it, I'm not lifting in my jeans."

Alex went over to his duffel bags and tossed her a pair of his boxers. "Try these."

Mad caught them, tugged the things on her smooth legs

and the three of them hit the weights. They'd been at it for about twenty minutes when there was a knock on the shop's door.

"It's open," Alex called out while he spotted Mad on some bench presses.

Cassandra walked in and froze, as if she'd stepped into the wrong place. Then she looked away wildly, eyes bouncing around.

Mad released the bar and sat up.

"Hi, Cassandra—" Alex didn't get further than that.

Cassandra's words trampled over his, coming out of her mouth in a rush. "Joy's been trying to reach you. Your phone's bouncing to voice mail."

"I turned it off."

Man, she totally refused to meet his eyes.

"Well, Joy would like you to come over for dinner tonight. She and Gray will be arriving in a couple of hours, and Frankie and Nate are due later this afternoon. I'm sure your…guest is welcome. And, Spike, you're invited as well. Six o'clock." She headed for the door. "You might want to call your sister. Anyway, that's all. Will you excuse me?"

"Cassandra, wait—"

She left so quickly, he didn't have time to finish.

"I'll be right back," he muttered as he grabbed his cane. Outside, the cold air bit into the bare skin of his chest. "Cassandra!"

Usually that tone of voice could stop a sailboat in a stiff breeze, but she just kept going.

"Goddamn it," he muttered, focusing on the ground so he didn't fall on his face.

He caught up with her just as she pulled back the plastic

flap over White Caps' kitchen doorway. She halted only because he grabbed her hand.

"Will you stop already! What the hell is the problem?"

Cassandra glanced over her shoulder at him. "There is no problem. Whatsoever."

She looked terrible, he realized. Dark circles under her eyes. Hollows under her cheekbones that he hadn't seen before. She was pale as salt, too.

"Cassandra," he said gently, "are you all right? You look sick."

"I'm fine. Please let me go."

Her listless voice lit off the back of his neck, and his nape tingled so badly he had to use his free hand to rub it.

"Cassandra, what's going on?"

Flat green eyes shifted away. "Please…let… Oh, God—"

She clapped her hand across her mouth, doubled over and gagged.

"Cassandra!" What the hell was she doing coming to work if she was sick? "For God's sake, let me take you back to Gray's."

She shook her head sharply, her ponytail flopping over one of her shoulders.

"Just leave me alone." Before he could say anything more, she cut him off. "If you don't get out of the way, I will throw up on your shoes. You are, quite literally, making me sick. Leave. Now."

Alex recoiled and dropped his hand from hers.

With a hoarse cough, she stumbled over to the Porta Potti.

Dizzy, still nauseated, Cass stepped out into the fresh air and breathed deeply. It didn't help. The sickly-sweet smell of the john clung to the insides of her nostrils like a coat of paint, spurring on her stomach's rebellion.

She went inside the house, turned on the propane heater and sat down on a board suspended between two sawhorses. She found that if she was motionless, the queasiness faded. Which was a good thing. The crew was due to arrive in about a half hour.

"Cass, baby?"

She winced and glanced over as Spike came through the plastic flap. He was smiling, but his eyes were razor sharp.

Great, she thought. Alex had sent reinforcements.

"Guess what?" the man said.

She took a deep breath. "What?"

"This is your lucky day."

"You can't be serious."

"I am. You're going to let me take you back to Gray's."

"And that makes me lucky, how?"

"Because if you come with me, Alex won't call an ambulance. I have five minutes to walk out of this house with you. Then he's dialing."

"Spike, no offense, but you've lied to me before."

"Maybe. But I'm not lying now."

She met his yellow eyes for a long moment.

"Come on, honey," he said softly. "Let me take you home."

Feeling like a fool, but not willing to run the risk of throwing up in front of her crew, she reached into her backpack and took out her cell phone. She dialed and when Ted answered, she asked him to ride hard on the plumbers. When she hung up, she didn't look at Spike, but got to her feet.

"Let's go," she muttered.

* * *

Cass slept most of the day. She couldn't stomach any-thing more adventurous than some of Libby's chicken broth for lunch, but by the time five o'clock rolled around, she was able to force herself out of bed. A shower perked her up a little and she slipped into a black sheath of heavy silk. She put on some makeup and did her hair. Threw on a pair of earrings.

She felt like she had to gird herself for the party.

By the time she walked into the living room, everyone else was there. Nate and Frankie were by the fire, their dark heads together. Joy was pouring some Perrier for Spike and laughing. Gray and Alex were talking.

Where was—

"That is a fabulous dress," Madeline said.

"Thank you."

The other woman was dressed in black slacks and a black turtleneck and she looked drop-dead gorgeous. Worse, her smile was open, engaging, as if she was hoping to talk. To be friends.

Cass searched her mind for something to say. "So it's very cold, don't you think?"

The weather. How original.

Madeline nodded. "And, man, the snow is everywhere. I've forgotten how much they get up here. I was crazy to take the Viper, but I love that car. With so much of my time being spent on the ocean, I don't get to drive it enough."

Gray and Alex came over. Cass faded to the edges of the group, looking around the room until she'd memorized where every piece of furniture was. She felt Alex watching her, but couldn't meet his eyes. She just didn't want to deal with all the emotions she was feeling, and if that made her a coward, fine. Paint her yellow.

Abruptly he went over to Spike and said something to him. Spike left and came back with two large, thin presents that were wrapped with what looked like mathematical precision.

Alex raised his voice. "Since we're all here, I have something I want to give Frankie and Joy. Spike, prop them up on the couch, okay?"

When the two gifts were against the sofa cushions, Alex checked the back of one and motioned his sisters forward.

"Frankie you're on the left. Joy, the right."

He stepped to the side.

"What is it?" Frankie asked, staring at hers.

"See, that's the thing with presents. You have to open them."

"Who goes first?"

"Together. I want you to do it together. Sorry there are no ribbons. I couldn't find any I liked."

Frankie and Joy ripped the things open. And then just stood, staring.

Cass leaned from side to side, trying to see what he'd given them.

Alex cleared his throat awkwardly. "All right, maybe it wasn't a good idea. But see— Here, move out of the way."

Cass gasped. The gifts were beautifully framed sets of sailboat drawings.

Their father must have done them, she thought, putting her hand to her throat.

"These are Dad's," Alex said. "I've gone through all of his plans and when I saw these two boats, I thought of you." He eased himself down on the floor. "This one, Frankie, is a schooner, a three-master. She'll take care of you. She's the one you want when you have your crew with you and you're in a storm. She's stable, she's responsive, she's beautiful. She'll never let you down. And her lines…just perfect." He turned toward the other. "And, Joy, see this one, she's the one you want when it's just you and your woman and the two of you are going out at twilight. She's a dream to captain because she's maneuverable so she'll let you enjoy the beauty of the ocean and share it with someone even if you're at the helm. She's a quiet ocean kind of girl, but she's no dummy. You need to get home quick and she'll take you as fast as the wind. She is totally reliable."

He sat back, looking at the drawings, hands on his thighs. "I tell you, when Dad drafted these, he had the two of you in mind. And all the markings are his. Well, except for the transom cross sections. I took the liberty of printing your names on them. I hope that's okay."

There was total silence in the room as Alex focused on the sailboats and his sisters stared at him.

Suddenly, he seemed to realize everyone had gone quiet, and he glanced over his shoulder, flushing. "Yeah, ah, sorry to monopolize the party. I just—" He coughed a little as he leaned on his cane to get off the floor. "Anyway…I wanted you to have them. Maybe you could, uh, hang them somewhere. If you wanted to."

There was a strangled sob. No, two of them.

Frankie and Joy launched themselves at him, throwing their arms around their brother. The sounds of crying were muffled against his sweater.

He stiffened and looked down at their heads with a frozen expression. Then he wrapped his arms around his sisters, pulling them closer, dropping his own head between theirs. Words were exchanged among the three, quietly.

Cass used her fingertips to wipe away tears. Needless to say, there wasn't a dry eye in the house. Even Spike was blinking furiously.

When the trio pulled apart, Frankie smiled as she mopped up her face with a cocktail napkin.

"This is so perfect," she said, sniffling. "Those gifts on tonight of all nights." She reached out for Nate and he took her hand, kissing her on the lips. "We're pregnant," she announced.

Joy clasped her hands to her mouth and teared up all over again.

Alex beamed, wrapped Frankie back in his arms and shook Nate's hand. There were all sorts of congratulations and well-wishing and weepy smiling.

The fabric of life, Cass thought as she watched. The basis of family.

When it was appropriate, she stepped in and kissed Frankie on the cheek. Then she made a quick excuse to Libby and left the room.

Her stomach was back on the roller coaster again, and she just wasn't up to sitting at the table. There was no way she could pretend everything was all right any longer, and in the midst of such happiness, she didn't want to be the pill in the corner with a frown on her face.

As she went upstairs, she put her hand on her flat belly.

She would never have what Frankie had, Cass thought. New life growing inside of her. The man she loved beaming and proud by her side. The happy announcement.

Empty. So very empty.

She wanted to cry, except it struck her as useless. So she

undressed, got into bed and closed her eyes. For some reason she was cold even though she was under the covers.

Alex stared at Frankie, feeling the smile on his face stretch his cheeks until they burned.

"So are you ready to be an uncle?" she asked.

"Yeah, I am."

"Oh, Alex, those drawings." Her eyes welled up. "That is the loveliest thing you've ever done."

Joy came up to him and took his hand. "Oh, Alex. They're so beautiful, so thoughtful. I never expected you—"

As his sister fell silent, he laughed a little. "Never expected me to what?"

"To know how much it would mean to us."

"What made you think of it?" Frankie asked.

He looked around. Everyone else was across the room, examining the plans in front of the couch. The three of them were alone.

Might as well finish it, he thought.

"You've had no help from me, no support, since the two of them died. And yet I come home, bashed up, needing all kinds of things, not the least of which being patience and understanding. You both took care of me. You never hesitated. I didn't deserve it. I still don't."

"Alex," Frankie cut in, "you're our brother—"

"How do you figure that? I left you two here all by yourselves. Not real brotherly. Not the mark of a good man, either." He cleared his throat. He was not going to cry. Damn it, he was *not*. "I'm going back out to sea."

He paused, taking in their stricken faces.

"But I'm going to return here more often, and I want to

help out. I know Grand-Em's care is expensive. I want to pay for it."

The cost would take a chunk out of what he earned. After all, sailing was a rich man's sport so the trophies were gorgeous, but the purses, even the America's Cup, were small.

"Alex, you don't—" As he stared at Frankie, she had the good sense not to argue.

He smiled and reached out to her belly.

"The next Moorehouse," he murmured.

What would it be like, he wondered, to put his hand on a woman's stomach and know that his son or daughter was nestled inside?

He thought of Cassandra. It was crazy, but he wished she wasn't on the Pill. And that they'd had unprotected sex every single night that she'd been up in Saranac.

He wished she were pregnant.

He glanced at the people by the couch and realized she was gone.

"Cass went upstairs," Joy explained. "She told Libby her stomach was still off."

"Do you know if she ate lunch?"

"Libby said only some of her homemade chicken broth."

"Then I'll take some more of that up to her."

Chapter Sixteen

When a knock sounded, Cass looked up from the novel she'd been skimming through.

She pushed herself a little higher against the pillows. "Come in."

The door swung open. The big, dark shape between the jambs could only be Alex and he was holding a tray on his palm like a waiter would. She wondered how he'd worked the knob with his cane.

But then, that was Alex. Great physical coordination.

He stepped into the room and kicked the door shut. "Before you say anything, I owe you this, remember? You brought me food when I wasn't doing too well."

She pulled the comforter up to her chin. Even though her flannel nightgown was as translucent as a two-by-four.

"You can leave it over there on the bureau," she said. "Thank you."

He ignored her and came to the bed. "You aren't going to let me feed you this soup, are you?"

"No, I'm fine."

He put the tray down and sat on the edge of the mattress, his weight causing a dip she had to fight not to get swallowed into.

"How are you feeling?"

"Fine."

His eyes narrowed. "No matter what I ask you, you're going to answer *fine,* right?"

"Alex—"

"Sorry, I didn't mean to bait you." He dragged a hand through his hair. "You've been working too hard."

"Not really."

"You need time off."

"I'm—"

"Fine. Yeah, sure. Listen, maybe you should take a few days for yourself. Or a week. Maybe you could even take a vacation. Go somewhere with—" Alex's face tightened "—O'Banyon or something."

God, she wanted to scream at him. "Alex, I'm going to give this one last shot and then I'm done, okay? There is nothing going on between Sean and me. That kiss you saw? It was the one and only time our mouths have ever met. I was…trying to feel something for him, but I didn't. That's the truth and I refuse to justify my business to you again."

Alex's brows came down and his eyes shifted away. He took a long slow breath. "You felt nothing?"

"No."

"O'Banyon did."

She shrugged. "I suppose."

Alex glanced at her. "He wants you."

"And he's a grown-up so he's willing to just be my friend. I don't— Oh, hell, Alex, what are we even talking about this for?"

He put his hands on his knees and shook his head. "Damn. Okay. I'm sorry that I read you and him wrong. I just assumed that... Well, the two of you look right together. So I just assumed..."

From out of nowhere, she remembered him leaning over that half-naked sex goddess, Mad Dog. While the woman was wearing his boxers.

Talk about looking right. The two of them were perfect together: beautiful, athletic, oozing raw sexuality. How he managed to stay away from the woman was a testament to his self-control because he and Mad were a hell of a combination.

And, even though she shouldn't bother, she felt for him; she really did. She was getting a good idea of how hard it was to want something you couldn't have, and he had wanted his Miracle for years.

"It's really tough, isn't it?" she murmured.

"What is?"

"Not being with the one you want."

He closed his eyes. "A living hell."

She stared at his strong profile. "Yes. Yes, it truly is."

As she looked at Alex, she thought about Reese. And remembered hearing his voice on the other end of the phone that night when his double life had finally been exposed.

Alex's woman would never have to worry about that. Had he actually been with his Miracle, had the two of them been in a relationship, he never would have taken Cass to bed. He never would have even *looked* at her.

The confidence she had in him made her ache. She'd thought fidelity was relatively unimportant to her, that security and safety were enough. She'd been so very wrong. For a marriage to work, it all had to be there. Love and passion and monogamy and...

"How much did you know?" she blurted out. "About Reese and the other women?"

Alex's head whipped around, shock peeling his eyelids back. "Excuse me?"

Talk about putting the man in a difficult position. "Sorry. I didn't mean to—"

"What did you just say?" he demanded harshly.

She cowered back, but then realized he wasn't angry, he was horrified.

No doubt because he was surprised that she knew what had been going on.

"You don't...you don't have to cover it up. I knew what was happening. I caught him red-handed one night about two years ago. Before then, I had suspected, but was never really sure."

Alex stared at her, his dark blue eyes unblinking. Maybe he was trying to form excuses in his head.

God, she hoped he didn't try and defend Reese or downplay the truth. She could understand Alex not wanting to get tangled up in his partner's marriage. But she wouldn't appreciate it if he glossed over the reality of the situation.

Alex's voice was stark. "He couldn't have— He couldn't have done that to you. How could he have done that?"

His expression was so incredulous, so disgusted, she

realized he truly knew nothing. Reese had hidden it from him, too.

She felt like apologizing and realized that was utterly ridiculous.

Alex grabbed her hand, squeezed it hard enough that her fingers hurt.

"How could he have been with someone else?" He shook his head and eased his grip. "I'm sorry. That's a BS question to ask you. I don't want to pry."

Actually, it was a relief to talk to someone about it. She'd kept the whole sordid mess to herself, and the fact that Alex hadn't known either made her feel less like a fool.

"I did wonder why and I did get angry, but I never confronted him. Now that he's gone, I wish I had. I despise myself for keeping quiet, because if I'd talked to him, maybe I wouldn't be so bitter now. Maybe I could have mourned him more honestly." She shifted her legs, emotions making her restless. "I will say that he was never disrespectful. He never brought it home. And he practiced safe sex. I found all these…condoms in the suitcases he used for travel."

She shuddered and took comfort by looking down at her hand in Alex's. Suddenly she wanted him to know everything. Her past was another secret she kept, and she wanted to out it, too. She was so damn tired of the social-gloss and stiff-upper-lip routine she'd been clinging to for as long as she could remember.

"Did you know he invented me? Well, *we* invented me. I come from absolutely nothing. No money. Mother and father who drank. I was lucky that I got into a state university on a scholarship, and when I graduated, I wanted to get as far away as I could from everything I'd known. I arrived in New York City with no illusions, and it was harder than I thought." She took a deep breath. "I got a temp job at an architectural firm and that's where I saw my future. I went to night school to get the degree. Reese was my first real client. He gave me access to his friends, helped start my firm, supported me socially. I married him eventually because it was the only thing he'd ever asked me for and I thought I loved him."

Cass felt something hit her face. When she wiped her cheek, it was wet. She rolled the tear back and forth between her thumb and forefinger until the thing disappeared.

"I stayed with him, even though I knew he was with other women on those sailing trips, because he loved me and he was a huge part of my life and— God, this is hard to say... I knew I didn't love him as much as I should have so I felt as though I couldn't really demand monogamy. It almost didn't seem fair." She sighed, trying to release the tension in her shoulders and belly. "I will tell you, never again. I won't...now I would never marry a man I didn't love down to my soul and I would expect him to be faithful. Always."

"I thought you were both totally in love," Alex said softly.

"We weren't. He loved me as best he could and it wasn't enough. I cared for him deeply and it wasn't enough. We were...very broken. Going along, going through the motions. He must have been unhappy, too, or he wouldn't have been with the others. Or at least...I'd rather believe that than think he was incapable of being true to someone he loved. Because that would be a serious failing, don't you think?"

She thought back to the first four years of her marriage, when she and Reese had tried to conceive. After the night of that phone call, she'd stopped being able to make love to him. It just hadn't felt right and he'd accepted her excuses.

God, her marriage really had been falling apart, hadn't it? More tears came to her eyes.

"What is it?" Alex asked.

"I didn't want him to die. Truly I didn't. I hear myself talking right now and I sound so bitter, but I think that's because I'm looking at the marriage honestly for the first time. And it's a shame that this is happening now, after he's gone. I don't think we would have lasted much longer together, but maybe we would have remained friends. He was a great friend. He could make me laugh—" She choked up.

Remembering the good times was so hard, but there had been some. A lot, actually.

Abruptly, she had an image of that aide in the nursing home and how awkward Alex had gotten when the woman had become emotional.

"Anyway," Cass muttered briskly. Her momentum was lost when she hiccupped and said nothing more.

Alex let go of her hand.

Oh, hell. She should have known not to go revealing her—

He shifted around so he was lying next to her. Then he pulled her against him.

Of course, that just made her want to weep in great gnashes and wails. And not because of Reese.

Kindness from Alex ruined her. Made her see yet again that whatever she'd felt for Reese, those emotions had been something entirely different from what a woman could truly feel for a man. Gratitude, respect, affection, warmth, it had all been part of a mix she had thought was love.

But she knew what had been missing now. The core of her had remained separate, apart from Reese.

Not so with Alex. Tragically.

As the great swell of emotion passed, she became aware of the smell of him, his aftershave mingling with a subtle scent that was only Alex. She felt his thigh running along hers and the thick pads of his pecs under her head. The warmth of him seemed to seep through the comforter and into her body.

She tilted her head up and looked at him. His eyes were closed.

God, his lips were so close. And so perfect. The lower one more full; the upper curved at the top.

Even though she knew it was a bad idea, she leaned in and kissed him softly. His lids flipped open and he jerked back.

He stared at her with hooded eyes, the midnight blue of his irises giving nothing away. Then he smoothed her hair back, pressed his lips to her forehead, and tucked her face into his chest.

Well, if that wasn't just about the nicest refusal she'd ever had.

A moment later, Alex got up from the bed. He kept his back to her as he walked over to the door. He opened it, stepped outside and shut it partway.

"Good night, Cassandra. I'll see you tomorrow, okay?"

She put her arm across her eyes. "Of course. Sure."

How could she have forgotten that his Miracle was downstairs?

"Captain?"

Alex looked across the interior of the Viper. He hoped Mad didn't want to talk about the dinner party. He didn't remember what he'd eaten, and had no idea what the bunch of them might have talked about.

"Captain?"

He shook himself. Evidently, his memory wasn't the

only thing he'd lost. His hearing had also checked out for the evening.

"Sorry?"

"I asked, what's doing?" She parked in front of the shop. He shrugged and opened the door. "Nada."

Palming his cane, he levered himself out. Snow was falling yet again and he wondered how in the hell she was going to get back to Manhattan in the sports car. His next thought was that he didn't have to worry. Mad could handle herself in any situation.

They went inside together and Mad took first crack at the bathroom. While she hummed that *Star Wars* theme and brushed her teeth, Alex stoked the potbellied stove and then waited at the desk, stewing.

No, he thought, wrong cooking parallel. He was steaming.

Alex was royally pissed. Angry enough to chew tin and spit nails.

If Reese had been alive, he would have done whatever he had to to get to the man—car, train, boat—and then he would have called his partner a bastard to the guy's face.

Would have been tempted to haul off and hit him.

It wasn't just that Reese had violated his marriage oaths and shamed Cassandra, although that alone was enough to shoot Alex into orbit. The sheer *stupidity* of the infidelity was offensive. If you had gold in your hands, why the hell would you go looking for stone?

"Captain, bathroom's free."

Alex nodded. And didn't get up.

Mad walked over and propped her hip against the desk. "You want to talk about it now?"

"No, I don't." But then the words just popped out. "Did you know Reese was cheating on his wife?"

"Yes."

Alex felt his eyes stretch. "God…damn. Why didn't I know?"

"You never went to the parties, Captain. That's when it happened. Everyone knew it. We assumed that's why he never brought her along and why she never met any of us. He wanted his lives separate, obviously needed to keep them that way."

Alex rubbed his palm over his face.

"There something going on between you and her?" Mad asked.

"No."

"You lying to me or yourself right now?"

"You."

"I won't say anything to the boys."

He got up, not trusting himself to say anything more. He was liable to spill his guts and he didn't want Mad having to keep so much from the rest of the crew.

"Thanks, Mad."

He went into the bathroom and tried to do a scrub job on his brain as he brushed his teeth. The former didn't work, but he was so furious his chompers were gleaming by the time he was finished.

Probably had stripped off half his enamel in the process.

When he came out, Mad was getting into her sleeping bag. She was wearing that sports bra and underwear combination again only this time the two halves were navy blue.

He thought of Spike that morning, looking so completely overwhelmed when the two of them had met. The guy's struck-stupids had persisted throughout the evening. He'd watched Mad the whole time, his lips zipped and his eyes super-focused. It was a total social reversal. At the New

Year's Eve party, Spike had been full of the yakkies around women. But with her, he was about as talkative as a ficus.

"So, Mad, I think you have an admirer," Alex said as he got into bed.

She cocked an eyebrow while punching her pillow into shape. "Yeah?"

"Spike likes you."

Mad grinned and settled herself on her side. Her eyes twinkled. "Oh, God, I really like him. He's got such a terrific edge to him…you know, that slightly dangerous thing. Too bad he's so shy."

Shy? Spike wasn't shy, he was enthralled. "I don't think that's why he's quiet."

"You know, it's too bad we don't need a cook. The rest of the boys would get a kick out of him. He'd fit right in with us."

Alex shook his head ruefully. How could she be so clueless?

"Mad, you're missing my point. He *likes* you. He's attracted to you."

She stared at him for a moment, the merry grin leaving her face. Then she slashed her hand through the air. "Yeah, whatever."

Mad turned on her back. Shut him out.

"Mind if I ask you something?" he said.

"Anything, Captain."

"It's personal."

"So."

"Do you like men?"

She looked over her shoulder at him and laughed. "All my friends are men, I work with men, I live with men. Of course I like them."

"I mean, sexually."

"Oh." Her eyes shifted away from his. "I—ah, I don't know. I've never had one before."

He smiled. "Don't feel awkward about it, for God's sake."

"Well, I guess I figure I'm a little unusual."

"You aren't. And I sure as hell don't care that you're a lesbian."

Her eyes shot back to his. She cleared her throat. Good Lord, was Mad Dog Maguire blushing?

"Captain, I'm not— I don't like women like that."

Alex frowned. "So if you've never been with a man and you're not a lesbian, what—"

"I'm a virgin, okay? I'm a professional athlete who's one of the best navigators in our sport who just happens to have never had sex. It's no big deal, you know." She grimaced and put her hands to her face. "God, are we really having this conversation? 'Cause I kind of hope this is a bad dream."

Alex could only stare at her.

"Stop staring at me, Captain."

"Sorry, it's just…a little bit of a surprise, that's all."

"Yeah, well, I'm not contagious or anything. You can't catch inexperience from me," she muttered.

"Jeez, Mad. I just figured…I mean, you're so comfortable with your body, so confident in yourself—"

"And you think I can't be all that and a virgin, too?"

"You're absolutely right."

"Look, just don't tell the boys. I don't have anything to hide, but there's no need to broadcast this kind of private stuff."

"It's no one's business but yours, Mad."

She laughed a little. "Thanks, Captain. Guess we're even, aren't we? One secret for another."

"Yeah. We're even," he murmured.

Alex eased onto his back, thinking of the other reason why he'd been so distracted over dinner. His one-time-only vow had been on the verge of disintegration the moment Cassandra had kissed him with such delicate inquiry. When he'd left her room, his body had been humming with sex. So much so, he'd had to wait a little before he could rejoin the party. It was either that or show off an obscenely prominent erection.

Never had his self-control been so fallible than with Cassandra.

Chapter Seventeen

Cass woke up the next morning and couldn't get out of bed. She was queasy and feverish and teetering on the brink of a decision she wished she didn't have to entertain. Even in the hypothetical.

She glanced at the clock to see what time it was, saw the congealed soup Alex had left on the bedside table and barely made it to the bathroom in time.

When she got back, a quick phone call to her office in New York was all it took. Jay Dobbs-Whyte, one of their younger associates, was going to come up and relieve her from the White Caps renovation.

She'd never had to leave in the middle of a project for personal reasons before. Ever. Once she started something, she finished it.

But after last night she needed some time to herself. She

wasn't concentrating at the site. Her health was suffering. And even if she forced herself to work, she was going to be next to useless if her stomach wouldn't let her get out of the bathroom.

Jay was going to drive up from the city tomorrow. She would take him through the house and then she would leave. All she had to do was tell Frankie and Joy. Which was going to kill her.

But she couldn't go on like this.

Cass got up, took a shower and was dismayed to learn that Frankie and Joy and their husbands had left already. She called their cell phones, got voice mail and left messages to the effect that she was turning the project over to a trusted colleague because she had health issues. She urged them to call her so she could explain the situation in greater detail.

Such detail not to include how she felt about Alex.

While she drove over to White Caps, she braced herself for seeing the shop. And she did a good job not dwelling on it as she went by, though she couldn't help looking at the glossy black Viper nestled up tight to the barn. The thing looked like part of a car ad in a magazine, so sleek and flashy against all the pristine snow.

Parking the Range Rover in her usual space, she got out and heard the men talking.

"Hey, boss!" Ted called over to her. "Glad you're here. We got a problem with the upstairs bath."

Getting swept up in the work actually helped, and except for a revulsion to lunch, she kept herself together. When three o'clock rolled around, she told the men what to expect from Jay and was touched as they seemed sorry she was leaving. After the crew had pulled out, she went back to Gray's and headed straight for her tub.

Her body was achy, and she ran the water as hot as she could make it. Sinking into the claw-footed thing of beauty made her moan with relief. Muscles that had been screaming tight all day long relaxed in a rush as she sank into the warmth. When there was a knock on her bedroom door, she was frustrated by the interruption.

"Cass? It's Libby, may I come in?"

"Sure, let me get out of the tub."

Except her body wanted to stay right where it was so negotiating her way free of the bath was a project. As she drew on a terry-cloth bathrobe, she couldn't wait to get back in.

Walking through her room, she had a wonderful feeling of dislocation, as if she were floating, a buoy in calm water.

"Hi, Libby," she murmured as she opened the door.

"I just wanted—" The woman frowned. "Are you okay? You look awfully pale."

"I feel fine." Cass swayed, that gentle, billowing sensation surging throughout her body. "I feel…lovely."

Then she fainted.

Alex and Spike left the nursing home together, and both of them were quiet as they got into the Honda. Actually, neither of them had said much since they'd left the shop about an hour before.

"You want to get something to eat?" Spike asked.

"Sure."

"Silver Diner?"

"Yeah." Alex stretched his arms, feeling the burn in his pecs. "I could use a blue-plate special or two after that workout we had this morning. You were a hard driver."

Spike shrugged and started the car. "No more than you were."

"Or Mad."

"Yeah, she's, ah, strong." Spike eased the Honda out of their parking spot. "How long is she staying?"

"She's left."

Spike's head jerked, as if he'd wanted to flip the thing around and had fought the impulse. "When?"

"After we finished this morning."

"Oh. Cool."

They were on the other side of town, closing in on the diner, when the man cleared his throat.

"Can I ask you something about her?"

Alex looked over. "Yeah, sure."

"Is it true that she's some kind of heiress or something? I mean, that's what Gray said."

"Val-U-Mart Supermarkets."

Spike whistled under his breath. "Wow."

"She's really down-to-earth, though. Viper notwithstanding." Alex frowned. God, Spike was so tense, he was about to snap the steering wheel right off the damn drive shaft. "Hey, buddy, what—"

"Listen, Lex, about heading to Blue Mountain Lake. I'd like to drive you. You free tomorrow?"

Nice evasive maneuver, Alex thought. And since he didn't appreciate it when people crawled up into his business, he let the subject stay changed.

Even though where their conversation had landed was an awkward spot for him. He wasn't sure why he'd even put the idea of the trip out there. He knew he wasn't going to end up building boats, for God's sake. He'd promised Mad he was coming back. He *wanted* to come back.

He was about to tell Spike to forget it when his neck started tingling. He reached up and rubbed the damn thing.

What the hell, he thought. It didn't hurt to just go up and talk to the guys. Conversation didn't mean anything.

He glanced at Spike. "Tomorrow's good for me. Thanks."

His cell phone went off.

When he shut the thing, his hands were shaking. "Cassandra passed out. Take us to Doc John's. Right now."

As Cass sat on an exam table in a flimsy little cotton gown, she felt as though she was in good hands. Doc John was in his fifties and looked like the kind of person you'd want to have on the other end of a stethoscope. He was as calm and steady as a mountain. About the size of one, too, with his woodsman's build. His clinic was housed in an old Victorian, and Cass was pretty sure she was being examined in what had once been a sitting parlor.

He smiled as he wrote down her weight and temperature.

"Is there any chance you could be pregnant?" he asked.

The question shocked her. "Uh, no."

"Have you been intimate with anyone lately?" Evidently, the blush that hit her face answered his question. "Maybe I'll just take some blood so we can rule it out, okay? I'll also check some other things. Thyroid and liver functions, iron levels, that kind of stuff."

"Fine with me. But I'm telling you, I'm not pregnant. My husband and I tried for years."

"Did you ever get a fertility assessment done?"

"No need to. He fathered two children with his first wife. It was me."

Doc John made a noncommittal noise and motioned

across the room. "Have a seat in that chair, if you don't mind. I'm going to draw the sample myself."

When he was finished taking the blood, he wrote her name on a label and wrapped it around the tube.

There was a commotion outside, voices rising sharply.

Doc John ignored the noise. "So here's what I think. You're exhausted. You haven't been eating enough. And you overdid it with the hot water in the tub, which was why you passed out. How's that for a diagnosis?"

She smiled a little. "Nothing that I hadn't guessed."

"Then I'm really going to knock your socks off with my prescription. Go home. Take some time off. Sleep until you can't stand to have your eyes closed for a moment longer and then stay in bed for another day. I'll send the blood out. Results will be back in forty-eight hours. Sound good to you?"

Cass nodded. "I was going to take a little break, anyway."

"And now you have a note from the doctor."

She smiled and gave him her cell phone number, thinking she'd be back in New York by the time the lab results came in.

"Thanks, Doc John."

"My pleasure. Call me anytime if you have questions." He shook her hand and left.

As she got dressed, there were more raised voices in the hall. When she stepped outside, she was surprised to come face-to-face with Alex.

And downright shocked when she got a look at him.

He was white as the wall behind him, and he was being restrained from going into her exam room by Spike.

Libby must have called him.

"What's wrong with you?" Alex demanded.

"Nothing."

"You passed out."

"Because I was in the tub too long. It's no big deal."

"You look like hell."

As Spike cursed, Cass felt the tickle of hysteria rise in her throat. "Well, thank you. How kind of you to point that out. Now, where is Libby?"

"She left. I told her we'd take you home."

"Fine. Let's go."

Cass turned and headed for the main door, wondering if she was ever going to feel like herself again.

As soon as the three of them pulled up to the mansion, Libby came out of the house and embraced Cass.

"Are you all right?"

"Exhaustion. Nothing more," Cass murmured as they went inside.

Alex waited until she and Libby got caught up. Then he pointed at the stairs as if he had a right to. As if Cass were his responsibility.

Which was absurd.

Still, she wasn't going to argue with him in front of Libby. In fact, she wasn't going to argue with him at all. She knew for a fact her bedroom door had a lock on it, and she was going to use the damn thing.

She quickly mounted the steps, but he was faster than usual, as if he knew what she was thinking. When she got to her room, she tried to shut her door in his face, but he stopped her easily.

By putting his whole body in the way.

"Alex, will you leave me alone?"

"No."

"Why?"

He shoved the door wide and walked in. "You can't take care of yourself, obviously. So someone better worry about you."

"Yeah, well, it's not going to be you. We already covered this, remember? Not your problem."

"Anyone else volunteering for the job? Aside from O'Banyon, I mean?"

She threw up her hands. "You're insane, you know that? Does Madeline know how nuts you are?"

He shut the door. "Yes, she's been under me for years."

Oh, there was a terrific image. "Alex, will you just—"

He grabbed her upper arms. "You scared the hell out of me. I walked into Doc John's and could barely see I was so terrified."

That shut her up. "Why?"

He opened his mouth. Clamped it shut. Tried the whole talking thing again. "Ah, hell, Cassandra. I don't want you to be sick. And I don't want you to be unhappy. I don't…"

He dropped his hands, looking curiously helpless.

Abruptly her energy burst left her, just evaporated into the air, leaving her tired and tender. She went over and sat on the bed.

"Alex, just go," she said quietly.

He didn't. He came over and lowered himself to the mattress, stretching his leg out in front of him. In the silence he picked up his cane and twirled it slowly in one hand, like a baton. Her eyes latched on to the movement. The lazy circling of the handle had a hypnotic effect, like the slow spinning of a watch dial's third hand.

He cleared his throat. "Last night, after you told me about Reese, I got so angry I wanted to put my fist through a wall. I just… I believe every word you said, but can't believe it happened, you know? I can't fathom why a man would do that to any woman he was married to, but especially to you. It's damn appalling, it really is. If he were alive today, I would be yelling at him right now."

She glanced over. And tried not to love him even more.

He was so full of honor and decency under that gruffness, she thought. A true man of his word.

How she adored him.

"Madeline is a very lucky woman," she murmured.

He frowned, the cane stopping. "Huh?"

Cass waved her hand, trying to wipe the words away. "Nothing."

He shifted to the side, regarding her as if she were crazy. "You think Mad and I are…"

"She's your Miracle, isn't she? And you can't be with her because she's a member of your crew. That's the why of it, right?"

Alex stared at her and then laughed a little. "No. Mad's good people and I'd go through hell for her. But there's nothing like that going on. Never has, never will."

"Oh."

Then who was she?

An awkward quiet stretched between them.

"Well, thank you for your concern this afternoon," Cass said, trying to get him to leave. Trying to end things.

She should tell him she was returning to New York, she thought.

Cass looked up. And stopped breathing.

Alex was staring at her with an absorption that made her feel marked, his navy eyes fixated, penetrating.

He leaned into her, her name coming out of him on an exhale.

She closed her eyes as Alex kissed her cheek. She expected him to pull back right away. Instead, he kissed her again, a little lower. Then lower still.

Then his mouth was on hers.

His lips were soft. So very soft. She opened her eyes a little. His massive shoulders were turned toward her, his big body pivoted on his hips. He kissed her again. Gently.

When his tongue came out and flicked across her lower lip, she broke the contact.

"Why are you doing this?" she groaned. "I thought it was just once. You told me it was just once."

While he pulled back and rubbed his face, her eyes drifted down his body and focused on his need. "You want me."

He looked down at himself. Tried to cover up with his hands what was showing through his jeans.

"Yeah. I do."

"Enough to break your once-only rule?"

He cursed, a vile word that cut through the quiet room. "You don't need to ask me that."

"Why not?"

"Because you know the answer." His eyes shot to hers as he deliberately rearranged his erection.

"Last night," she murmured, "when you left, was it because you wanted me then, too?"

"Yes."

Sweet relief poured through her. To know that he still wanted her, still needed her, even if his Miracle—

Cass bit her lip and stared at his mouth.

She knew she was falling deeper into a spiral that was only going to bottom out with her in pieces. But still, if she could have him one last time, she'd take him. Even though it would just hurt her more later.

Except, the start would have to come from him. She wasn't going to get turned down again. She knew what she wanted. He was the one who was on the fence, trapped between where his body wanted to go and where his heart wasn't.

Their eyes met and held.

Kiss me again, she willed. Kiss me. Now.

Alex got to his feet and left.

As the door closed, she felt as though she'd been stabbed in the chest.

Stupid. Stupid…idiot.

Going home was *such* the right thing to do, she thought, as she peeled her clothes off.

She went into the bathroom and had a quick shower, careful not to make the water too hot. When she got out, she wrapped a towel around herself and went back into the—

Cass froze.

Alex was in the bed, propped up on the pillows, his bare chest resplendent. With one fluid, powerful movement, he drew the covers back and revealed his nakedness, welcoming her to lie beside him.

"I had to tell Spike to go home," he explained.

Chapter Eighteen

Alex watched, heart in his throat, as Cassandra's gleaming green eyes drifted down his body. He knew it was wrong to be with her, because she deserved to know the whole truth, but he would tell her everything tomorrow. Tonight he couldn't fight what he needed anymore and he prayed she would let him inside.

Her towel dropped to the floor.

She came toward him, her body moving slowly, gracefully.

As she slid in between the sheets and up against him, he let the covers fall over them both. He pulled her body on top of his, tangling his legs in hers, wrapping his arms around her. He kissed her shoulder, her neck, her mouth. With restless, desperate sweeps, he smoothed his hands over her back and her hips and her bottom.

"I want this to be good for you," he said, shoving her

hair aside and going for her ear. "But I'm so hungry. I just need... I have to be with you."

She said something in a husky, sexy voice, but he didn't catch the words because he was flipping her over and settling himself on top of her. Lacing his fingers through hers, he held on to both of her hands and squeezed as he kissed her deep enough so he lost his breath. The suffocation increased his pleasure, cranking the heat up so high his whole body, not just his erection, burned. He kissed her harder, feeling as if he was dying and desperately wanting the sweet death she gave him, wanting it until he shook. Raw, wild, unworthy, he needed her, he loved her, in spite of his failings.

And she wanted him, too. He could feel it in the surging feminine body under his hard contours; in the gasp she let out as he moved down to her breast and took her nipple between his lips; in the flush that bloomed over her satin skin.

In a frantic, jerky movement, he reared up onto his knees and threw off all the bedding. Looming over her writhing body, watching her look at him with greed, he was half-mad with the wanting.

But he stopped. "Cassandra..." His voice was little more than a growl. "I'm...sorry."

She arched, throwing her breasts up, knotting the sheet under her in frustration with her hands. Her legs shifted restlessly.

"For what?" she moaned.

"I can't stop. I should, but I can't."

"I don't want you to."

"You will later. You will wish we hadn't done this. Any of it."

She let go of the fists she'd made in the sheets and reached up for his body. "I don't want to think about later. I only want to know now."

Cass stared up at Alex's perfectly beautiful body. His perfectly aroused body.

His need for her looked as if it must have been painful, it was so swollen, so stiff.

But his eyes were haunted. She shook her head.

"Don't police my feelings, Alex. Be with me if you want to, but let me worry about myself, okay?" When he stayed still, her voice turned hard. "What are we doing here, Alex? I'm clear with what I want. Is it yes or no for you?"

He answered by leaning down and running his hands up the inside of her thighs. He coaxed her legs apart, and she arched, ready to have him lie between them.

The sensation of his mouth on her hip was a shock. And so was the way he lowered himself to the mattress, his great arms slipping beneath both her knees, the width of his shoulders lifting her legs, separating them. The sight of his massive torso under her slender thighs made her feel so very small and it turned him into some great male animal, stretched out before her most vulnerable place.

Something chilly fluttered through her. Not fear, because she knew without a doubt that he would never hurt her. It was just…the intimacy seemed a little overwhelming.

As if he sensed her hesitation, he rubbed his head on her belly, his hair soft and silky. She could feel his breath on her skin, hot and moist.

"Will you let me do this, Cassandra? Will you let me know you this way?" He kissed her right below the navel and then licked the spot. "Because I want to. So badly. I'll be gentle, I promise. So very gentle." He nuzzled his face against her. "Please let me do this…nice and slow."

"Yes, Alex…"

His big hands splayed over her stomach, holding her down, as his mouth found her very center. She cried out at the contact of his lips, and he looked up at her, eyes shining out of the low angle of his face. He watched her as he pleasured her, taking her in two ways, with his languorous mouth and his hungry gaze.

"You are so beautiful," he whispered hoarsely. "Oh, sweet heaven…the honey of you…"

A wave of pleasure crested and sank her, throwing her body into contractions that tightened her from head to foot. In the midst of it, a heavy weight came down on top of her and then there was the sweet invasion of him, the awareness that he was sliding deeply within her, the glorious joining.

His head burrowed into the pillow next to hers as his body went through its erotic masculine dance. His breath punched out of him, the roar of it loud in her ear. She savored the slick sweat and the vibrant heat and the pounding power of him. Her hands went to his back and she held on as best she could.

When he reached his pinnacle, he called out her name. And spilled himself into her like wine.

It was sometime later when Alex craned his neck around and looked at the clock. Nearly midnight.

Time for him to go. It wouldn't be a good idea for both Cassandra and him to show up at White Caps in the same car in the morning. Not in front of all those workmen of hers.

He closed his eyes and put his head back down just so

he could relish holding her in his arms for a little longer. Then he slipped out of the bed and dressed quietly.

Leaning over her, he kissed her softly on the shoulder. He didn't want to wake her up, not given how exhausted she was.

Downstairs, he called Spike who, bless his heart, was in front of Gray's in ten minutes.

Alex got into the car.

"Thanks—" He frowned, pausing as he went for the seat belt. "'Scuse me, man. But those pants you're sporting. Are those what I think they are? Are those…jammies?"

"I was crashed when you called, okay? And there's nothing wrong with *Star Wars*."

Alex grinned. "For a twelve-year-old, maybe. I didn't know they even made that kind of thing in man-size. Do they have the little footies on them?"

Spike flipped a choice finger in the air and downshifted.

"Well, do they?"

"No."

"That is such a disappointment."

Spike pulled up to the workshop and Alex glanced at his friend. "Hey, thanks for not asking. You know, about Cassandra."

The man nodded. "No problem. I'm just glad you finally got it together."

Except they weren't really together.

And God knew, they were going to be worlds apart tomorrow, when he told her everything.

In an odd way though, he felt relieved. The hiding had gone on for so long that it had become a permanent condition in his life, like the color of his hair or his eyes. The realization that the end point had arrived was strangely liberating.

He would get over the feeling, he was damn sure of that. Because how Cassandra was going to react when he was through talking was not really an open question. She might have fallen out of love with her husband, but that didn't mean she'd want to keep making love with the guy who'd let him die.

And as for the news that he'd loved her from afar for years? He couldn't imagine that was going to go over any better. He was going to come across as an obsessed, dishonorable lunatic.

But telling her only part of the story wasn't an option. He had to let both halves loose because the two were inextricably linked. His love for her and Reese being lost to the sea were…one and the same in all the ways that mattered.

"Lex? You cool there, buddy?"

"Uh, yeah. See you in the morning."

"You betcha."

Chapter Nineteen

The trip to Blue Mountain Lake took longer than Alex had expected because the Norwich brothers had been psyched at the prospect of a partnership, and their excitement had been contagious. It was very possible that the three of them could work something out, and Alex was pumped from all the ideas spinning in his head. As the Honda sped south on the Northway, heading back toward Saranac Lake, he found it hard to remember why he couldn't be a sailor and a builder.

Then he shifted his leg under the glove compartment and was even more convinced he could do both. As the pain he now took to be normal sat up and knocked on his nerve endings, the sting made him think about the future.

He couldn't keep going in the sailing racket forever. A professional captain had a longer career horizon than other athletes, sure, but it was still a hard, rough life and his leg was going to be a permanent liability. No matter how much he rehabbed the damn thing, it was always going to be weak, and if he ever injured it again, he could lose the limb below the knee. All it would take was snapping that titanium rod out of place and he was done for.

Spike glanced at him. "You want to stop for eats somewhere on the way home?"

"Actually, I want to go directly to Gray's."

The grin that came back at him was all-knowing. "Am I going to get another one of those midnight calls again?"

Alex winced. "Yeah, about that, I hated dragging you out of bed."

"Come on, Lex, I'm just busting on you for fun. It's no biggie. I just don't want to hear about my intimate apparel, you feel me?"

"They had light sabers on them, buddy."

"So?"

"And R2D2."

"Yeah, and you can kiss my Wookie, dig?"

Alex threw back his head and laughed.

Twenty minutes later they pulled up to Gray's. The Range Rover wasn't there, but a white Chevy Suburban was parked in front.

Alex frowned. "Hold up, Spike, will you?"

He went to the front door and drove the brass knocker home a couple of times. Libby answered. The words they exchanged were polite, friendly.

And killed him. Just laid him out flat until he thought he was bleeding.

He went back and got into the car, hoping he'd numb out soon, praying that shock would set in.

"Take me home, man," he said roughly.

"What's doing?"

"She's gone. Back to New York. She's left the project. Take me home."

Cass opened the door to the Manhattan penthouse and breathed deeply. The place smelled as it always did: lemon wax and old wood. As she put her bag down, and heard the sound echo into the high ceiling of the marble foyer, she decided she was definitely going to sell the place. It was too big for her to live in alone and it had always been Reese's somehow, even though they'd bought it and furnished it together.

Cass shut the door and felt the darkness around her as a tangible thing, like heavy cloth or a thick fog. Drawn by the ambient light ahead of her, she walked through the grand living room, passing by the phenomenal stretch of windows with their sweeping view of Central Park. As she wandered aimlessly, the antiques and the furniture were nothing more than shadows, the extravagant draperies like ghosts, the sound of her footfalls and sighing a muffled fugue.

Absurdly frightened, she turned on all the lights, and not just there, but in every one of the fifteen rooms. Even though she had spent all her nights alone in the place since Reese had died, now she felt unsettled and isolated. Very much alone.

Eventually, she calmed down and had a bite to eat out of the freezer. Before she retired to bed, she went around and turned off the lights. When she got to the library, she stared at the portrait of Reese that hung over the marble fireplace. The painting was a very good one, executed by a master, and the eyes followed you.

Which struck her as appropriate. Because she suddenly had a lot to say and wanted his full attention.

"I love him," she told the portrait. "And, yes, it's more than what I felt for you."

Reese with his competitive nature would have wanted to know that, even if it had hurt him.

"I've finally figured out that I'm angry at you and frustrated with myself. And I've felt this way for a while."

In the silence, she stared at his familiar face, studying the cheeks and the eyes and the forehead and the silver hair.

Then she looked at his left earlobe. Seeing the little gold hoop he'd worn triggered a memory of something that had happened in the beginning of their marriage.

Reese had decided on his fiftieth birthday to get his ear pierced. He'd wanted to get a tattoo, probably because Alex had one, but he'd been smart enough to admit that getting some ink was probably a little too hard-core for him.

The two of them had gone to a suburban mall, to a Claire's boutique. He'd sat down on the stool, acting all macho and flirting with the woman who was going to do the deed. It was all kicks and giggles until she got out the piercing gun. One look at that thing and Reese broke out in a cold sweat. The excuses had started rolling, and before Cass had known what was happening, they were back out in the mall.

As they'd returned to Manhattan, he was unusually quiet in the car, and when they got home, he'd gone into his study. He'd come to bed very late and had woken her up, distraught. He'd wanted to try the piercing again. First thing in the morning.

Calming him down had taken some time and it had taken even longer before he could tell her what was wrong. He'd been worried that she wouldn't think he was strong enough to take care of her. Just because he'd balked at the boutique. She'd tried to reassure him, but he'd had none of it.

The next day they'd gone back to Claire's, and he'd come out of there with a stud in his lobe. Even though he'd trembled all the way through it.

She thought about the will he'd drafted. She was more than taken care of; he'd left her the bulk of his private estate. And he'd set up things so she had total control of the trusts, so she could have whatever she wanted, whenever.

Cass frowned, trying to remember what his last words to her had been. He'd called her before he'd set out with Alex that day of the storm. What had she talked about with him? An upcoming party in the Hamptons. Arrangements for a trip to Rome. But there was something else…

A limerick. He'd given her a limerick. How had it gone?

There once was a man on a boat,
Who had the whole ocean to float,
He went here and there, to find himself something at
which to stare,
When all along what he needed was home.

He'd laughed and said he didn't care that the last word didn't rhyme because he was taking poetic license. Then he'd hesitated. He'd told her he loved knowing she was home and safe because it gave him such peace. And then they'd ended the phone call with what had turned out to be their last goodbyes.

They had been warm ones, she realized with relief. She'd been touched both by what he'd said and the tentative tone in his voice. He'd known, she realized. He'd known that she was aware of what he was doing. And he'd had regrets.

Tears pooled and fell, but they were not hard to bear this time.

Her chest cavity had been swept clean of anger, the dark emotions leaving a calm acceptance in their wake. And that peace gave her the ability to remember other parts of him, other parts of them.

The fondness. The mutual respect. The caring.

"Oh, Reese. We tried, didn't we? And we would have remained friends when we'd split. That much I know."

As the grandfather clock chimed behind her, she wiped her face and went to the guest room she'd started staying in about a year ago. She fell into bed and slept for twelve hours.

Cass woke up hungry, but for some reason all she wanted was eggs. As they were the only thing that appealed, she had seven of them. Fried in butter.

God, how gross, she thought as she finished the last one and considered having an eighth.

Marie, her maid and dear family friend, arrived at ten, and Cassandra chatted with the woman for a while before taking a shower. Under the rush of water, the nausea came back, but then what could she expect considering she'd wiped out a henhouse for breakfast?

As she opened up her walk-in closet and tried to decide what to wear and how to spend the day, she heard a bleating noise from her purse over on the dresser. Her cell phone was ringing.

She dug it out. "Hello?"

Doc John's voice came across loud and clear. "Congratulations! You're pregnant."

Cass took the phone away from her ear and stared at it. Actually thought about shaking the thing a little.

"Hello?" he said in a tinny reverberation. "Can you hear me?"

She put the phone back to the side of her head. "I'm sorry, I can't be pregnant."

"You're going to need to see an obstetrician, and I'd like to call you in a prescription for prenatal vitamins. Also, you have to eat more. Find things you can stomach and start munching. Think high fat, lots of carbs. You need to put on some weight fast."

"But you don't understand, I can't get pregnant. I'm not pregnant."

"You are."

Cass thought about the nausea and exhaustion, but couldn't believe they were tied to a baby. They had to be from some sort of flu. After all, she and Alex had been together only twice, well, three times really. The first of which being only about three weeks ago. So it was way too early for morning sickness—

Wait a minute. There had been that time right before Christmas. Which was like, what, six weeks ago? Except he hadn't—

"Cassandra? Are you still there?"

"Ah, yes. I think so. I'm not sure."

He laughed softly. "Do you have any questions for me?"

How much time do you have? she thought.

"I...I'm not up north," she said, "so don't bother with the vitamins. I'll see my doctor today. Uh, thank you."

As soon as she hung up, Cass called her own internist who said she could come in at twelve-thirty. When she put the phone down, she went back into the bathroom and dropped the towel. Standing naked before the mirror, she smoothed her hand over her belly.

What if…

Her eyesight went blurry.

She'd thought she'd accepted the fact that she couldn't have children. She honestly had.

But now a door that she'd assumed was locked forever had unexpectedly opened. What was on the other side was…high voltage joy, bright and warm as sunlight.

Okay, now she was really crying.

Were the weepies another sign of pregnancy? she wondered as she sniffled.

A baby. She was going to have a—

Cass thought of Alex.

Oh, God.

She closed her eyes, happy tears drying up instantly. What was Alex going to think?

When Cass let herself back into the apartment that afternoon, she said hello to Marie and went straight to her room. It didn't take her long to pack an overnight bag.

She was six weeks along. Six weeks pregnant with Alex Moorehouse's child.

Somehow that first time they'd been together, enough of him had gotten into her…and biology had taken care of the rest.

She was driving back to Saranac Lake because it was the only thing to do. News like this was not something you wanted to spring on a man over the phone, and explaining it all was going to be tough. She was pretty sure he was going to be horrified.

But she wasn't. She was carrying the baby of the man

she loved. So even if she couldn't have Alex, she would always have a part of him.

Cass paused while stuffing a flannel nightgown into her Vuitton duffel. Funny, it had never occurred to her that Reese might be the reason she hadn't gotten pregnant before. The fact that he'd been twenty years younger when his first children had been conceived just hadn't seemed particularly significant.

She checked the clock. It was almost two. If she made good time, she'd be up at the lake by six-thirty. She'd stay overnight and come right back.

She'd been told if she wanted to keep the baby, she better get eating and get some rest. She had every intention of following that prescription to the letter. There was no way in hell she was doing anything to jeopardize the gift she'd been given.

She told Marie she would be back in the middle of the following day and hurried out of the penthouse. Punching the elevator button, she waited, tapping her foot. She was in a rush to go up to the lake, do the talking and return home.

The doors opened.

She staggered back against the wall in the hallway. "Alex…"

Chapter Twenty

Alex reached out, thinking Cass was about to faint again. "Are you okay? You've gone white as snow."

"What—are you doing here?"

"I came to see you." He eyed her bag. "Look, you're obviously going somewhere, but can we talk? I won't take long."

"How did you get to Manhattan?"

"Spike. He's waiting downstairs."

"Oh, of course."

Her eyes latched on to his face and she stared at him in the strangest way. As if he were…he didn't know what. He couldn't decide whether her eyes were glassy or reverent.

"Cassandra? Can we go inside?"

"Of course. Come in."

Alex took a quick look around as he went through the

door. He'd never been in their penthouse before and wasn't surprised it was tricked out like a museum.

But the decor didn't interest him because he was focused on Cassandra. Her hair was pulled back in a ponytail and she was wearing her parka. As if she were going to the country.

He knew better than to think she'd be coming to see him and wondered where she was off to. Not asking was killing him, but he reminded himself that it wasn't his business, even though he wished liked hell it was.

"Marie," she called out. A dark-haired woman came around a corner. "Perhaps you'd like to take the rest of the day off?"

Marie nodded and smiled. *"Merci, Madame."*

Cassandra said something in French to the woman. Then she lifted her hand, indicating an ornate doorway.

"Let's sit in here."

The room they went into was a nice parlor kind of thing. Silk couches, big view, grand piano.

God, he hoped he could get through this in one piece.

Cassandra sat down on a chair, arranging herself as if she were in a ball gown, not slacks and a sweater. Her innate elegance astounded him, drew him, floored him. He was struck by the need to fall to his knees in front of her.

Instead he did his best to play real man even though he felt as if he was falling apart. He took the couch, stretching his leg out.

"Alex—"

"Cassandra—"

They both shut up.

He took the lead in ending the silence. "I need to tell you about…Reese. And that night. In the storm. I know you have an idea of what happened, but I want you to know everything."

Cassandra went perfectly still.

"The storm came up on us hard and fast. We'd expected bad weather, but not on that kind of magnitude. No one did. The barometer kept falling and falling and we'd decided to head back to shore when we got caught in the hurricane. We weathered the first hour or so fairly well, but then our mast snapped in half from the wind. Reese went aft to try and cut the sail loose because the gusts were grabbing it and pulling us off keel. He was struck in the shoulder by a loose piece of rigging. I saw him hit the deck, and then a wave came crashing over the bow. He didn't have his harness on and he couldn't find anything to hold on to. I scrambled to get to him. I grabbed his safety jacket, but it slipped and then I caught his hand. I…"

He stammered. Fell silent.

"Alex?"

He rubbed his face, bearing the horrible memories with no strength whatsoever. He felt as if he couldn't breathe.

"Alex, what is it? What happened?"

He looked at her. When he spoke, his voice was so thin, it was barely audible to his own ears. "I…killed him."

Cassandra's mouth opened slightly. "What? No, no, you didn't—"

He couldn't bear to look at her because he was afraid he was going to lose it. He put his head in his hands.

"Cassandra, I let the sea have him. I let him go. I let go…of his hand… I let go of his hand. I let it go… I let go…" He broke down completely, great sobs cutting through his chest, his body. There was no end to the weeping, to the hoarse words that wouldn't stop coming out of his mouth.

Eventually he lost his voice and the crying slowed.

He felt something grip his forearms and then his palms were pulled from his face.

Cassandra's green eyes were full of compassion as she stroked his cheeks.

"Oh, Alex…you couldn't have kept ahold of him. The wind, the waves, the tossing boat. The Coast Guard told me what it was like. He was taken from you. You didn't let go."

"I did! It happens in my dreams, over and over again. I feel him slipping and…I just let him go."

"Shh…it's all right. I don't want you to blame yourself. You had no reason to want him dead—"

"I did. I do."

Cassandra recoiled. "But why?"

He shrugged out of her hold. Got up and went to the window. "He had what I wanted. What I needed. Something I cherished…."

Cass watched Alex as he stood across the room. His back was straight, his legs braced. Against the yawning view of the city, he seemed as rigid as the skyscrapers beyond his broad shoulders.

"What did you want, Alex? What did he have that you wanted?"

He turned around. His face was bleak as an Adirondack winter. "You."

Cass frowned. Leaned forward a little. "Excuse— What? Me?"

"I…have…loved you since the first day I saw you. I've wanted you, I've obsessed about you, I've fantasized about you. You…you are my Miracle. I let him go…because I wanted you."

His words went into her ears, but her brain couldn't process them.

She shook her head. "No, that's not right. You didn't like me."

"I liked you too much."

"You stayed away."

"I had no choice."

"You… No, you—"

"I haven't been with a woman for six years, Cassandra. Because all I saw was you."

She rose from the floor. And then thought that sitting on the sofa was a good idea.

"You didn't know me."

"I didn't have to. When I saw the sea, I knew it was where I wanted to be. It was the same with you. One look in your eyes and I was lost. I'm like that. I know what I want and where I want to be."

Cass released her breath. "But when we were together. You stopped. And then you said only once. You—"

"I killed your husband. How could I take your body when you didn't know that?" He dragged a hand through his hair. "Except… Oh, God, I did make love to you. And not just once but again and again. I'm sorry. Not that I was with you, but because I wasn't honest with you."

She stared into space, jumbled pictures filtering through her mind.

"Just so we're clear," she said, "I don't believe you killed him. I think that's what you fear happened. But I'm willing to bet anything that you held on for dear life and his hand slipped out of yours."

"Cassandra—"

"What was the first thing you did after you felt yourself lose him?"

"I…I went for the flashlight."

"And what did you do with it?"

"I looked for him." Alex's eyes darkened to black. "I searched the waves…for a man in the water. I searched and called out his name and…"

"And what would you have done if you'd seen him? You would have gone after him, right? That's why you were looking for him. Because you wanted to save him." She shook her head. "Those don't sound like the actions of a killer to me."

Alex opened his mouth. When no words came out, he just nodded. A little.

"So you didn't kill him," Cass said strongly. "No matter what you think you feel for me—"

"I *know* what I feel for you. *I love you.*"

His face was grim, and his voice reverberated with conviction.

He honestly did love her.

Staring up at him, Cass was too stunned to speak. All she could do was look at him.

Say something, you idiot. The man you love loves you back. Say something.

Silence stretched out until the air grew tight between them.

God, she was just stuck. Caught in a morass of disbelief and hesitant, unexpected happiness.

Alex cleared his throat and started to back up toward the doorway.

"I'm sorry to dump all this on you," he said as he headed

out. "I just...wanted you to know. I don't expect you to understand. But I never want to—"

Say something.

"I'm pregnant," she blurted out.

Well, at least that got him to stop.

But let's just make sure he doesn't go anywhere, she thought.

Cass burst up off the couch, pounded across the room and threw her whole body around him.

Alex seemed utterly flabbergasted, but then his arms gripped her. When he would have separated them, she hung on so hard, she heard his neck crack.

"I love you, Alex. I love you, I love you, I love you... And you're going to be a daddy."

Chapter Twenty-One

Sean O'Banyon told his driver to pull over in the seventies on Park Avenue. "I'll be right back, Joey. Just going up to check on Mrs. Cutler."

"Yeah, sure, boss."

Sean opened the car door and waited for a hole between taxis that was big enough for him to shoot through. Cass was back in town, evidently. But the only reason he knew it was because he'd called Gray's after having gotten voice mail for three days straight.

Something was up and he was damn well going to find out what it was.

Pulling his dress coat around him, he jogged halfway across Park and paused at the median. That was when he saw the maroon Honda parked in front of Cass's apartment building with that spiky-haired guy in the driver's seat.

Sean hustled across the street, dodging a delivery truck and a bike messenger. When he hit the sidewalk, he went over to the car and peered inside.

Spike had put the seat back and was apparently snoozing, even though it must have been cold as a meat locker in there. Sean rapped on the window with his knuckle.

The man's eyes lifted slowly, the yellow gaze amused. As if he'd known who was looking into the car.

Sean opened his mouth but was cut off.

"Zoo animals have a weird life," the guy said, his voice muffled through the glass.

"Excuse me?"

"You know, getting stared at while they're in a cage. Freaky. I wonder if they think it's weird, too."

Okay, the man probably had a point. But Sean wasn't interested in a philosophical discussion right now.

"Listen, is Moorehouse up with Cass?" he said loudly so he was sure the words carried.

Spike put the window down. "Yeah. And don't think about getting in the way. He's got things he needs to say."

Sean frowned. "Are you threatening me?"

"Pretty much. Except I'll follow through on it. So I guess it's more like a promise, huh?"

Sean laughed. "I like a man's who's up-front."

"So you and I have something in common. Now, how about you return the favor. You going to be trouble?"

"If he hurts her, I'll put his head on a plate. If he's here to make nice, I'll be the first to shake his hand."

Spike nodded his head. "Good deal."

"How long you been here?"

"'Bout an hour."

Frankly, it was a surprise the guy wasn't a Popsicle. The

cold snap that had hit earlier in the week had stuck around, driving the temperatures into the teens.

Sean glanced over at his limo. "You think you're going to be here long?"

"Hope so."

"You got a cell he can reach you on?"

"Yeah."

"You want to get out of the cold? Have a drink or something? My place is about two blocks that way."

While he pointed to the right, he thought it might be fun to get to know this hard-ass guy. Sure as hell there was a story to him, and like the staunch Irishman he was, Sean loved a good story.

Spike put the window up and got out.

Damn, he was tall, Sean thought. There weren't a lot of men who could meet him square in the eye, but Spike sure could.

"Yo, Ricky?" the guy called out.

Richard, the doorman, poked his head out of the lobby. "Yeah?"

"I'm leaving her here, okay? Might be a while."

"Sure thing, Spike."

As they crossed Park Avenue, Sean said, "How do you know Richard?"

"Met him an hour ago."

"You got a way with people."

Spike smiled, a dark, mysterious grin. "Some of them."

Chapter Twenty-Two

Alex stirred and nestled in close to the warm woman lying next to him. His hand found her stomach and rubbed it in slow circles. He'd done that a lot while she'd slept, trying to come to terms with a kind of joy he hadn't known existed in the world.

Cassandra was carrying his child. And she loved him back. And they were going to get married.

From out of the bottomless bliss, he saw his father's face, and a memory came back, rising to the surface of Alex's mind. The two of them had been standing on the dock the night before Alex was due to leave for another one of his races.

He'd had no idea that he wasn't coming back anytime soon. He'd figured it was going to be the same as all the other departures. Four weeks gone, maybe six. He certainly hadn't planned on it being a final cut of sorts, the break that took him away from his family.

But his father had known. Somehow his father had known.

Alex heard his father's voice. "You know, son, life takes you a lot of places. Some good, some bad. I've always found that having a home somewhere makes the good better and the bad bearable. I hope you'll remember you can always come back here. No matter how far away you go, we'll always be here."

Alex had shrugged off the words with all the arrogance and self-possession of youth.

It was the last time he'd seen his father alive. Four years later the man had been dead. Alex's mother, too. Both at the hands of the water.

Alex thought of the horrible night on the sea with Reese.

Reese was gone, as well.

As he stroked Cassandra's belly, he felt a titanic shift in himself.

His woman stirred and lifted her head. "Good morning— Alex, what's the matter?"

"I'm not going out again," he said. "I'm not going back out there. I'm staying with you and the baby."

"What…the sailing? You're giving up the sailing?"

"Yeah. I am."

A pained relief hit her face, but then she shook her head. "No, Alex, you love the—"

"I love you," he said, kissing her. "The winning is cold and irrelevant compared to that. And nothing is worth the time away from you. Nothing."

There was no way his wife and his child were going to have to fend for themselves and worry about whether he was coming home. And he didn't want his sisters doing that anymore, either.

He was owning his own life from now on, not letting the need to compete drive him toward an ever-unreachable sunset.

Alex shifted his body to get even closer to Cassandra, feeling her soft skin brush up against his hard places.

One hard place in particular.

As her lids dropped and she started to smile, he laughed deep in his throat. The very male core of him was hungry for her again, in spite of the many times they'd reached for each other in the night.

But before his lips took hers, he pulled back. "Oh, no…"

"What?"

"Oh…hell. I left Spike down on the street."

Cassandra sat up. "We better—"

Alex's cell phone rang. Because Cassandra was closer to where his pants had landed, she leaned over and answered it. When she hung up, she was laughing.

"Spike doesn't want to talk to you, but not because he's mad. He doesn't want to disturb us. He's over at Sean's and perfectly well. The two of them had a grand time last night, and they want to meet us for lunch. And Sean is thrilled, as he put it, that we came to our senses. He wants to know when the wedding is and where."

Alex grinned. "You know, I might just warm up to that guy. And lunch sounds good."

Because he was going to need some help. He had an engagement ring to buy. Between Spike and Sean, he figured the three of them could take on the diamond district.

"Oh, and there's one other thing," Cass said as Alex pulled her back against his body, spooning himself around her.

He reached for her breast and nibbled on her shoulder. As she shivered and warmed under his hand, he murmured, "One more thing?"

"Spike said that Sean's more of a gentleman than you are."

"Oh, yeah?"

"Um, I guess Sean didn't make fun of his Wookie?"

Alex laughed and swept his palm down her body. "I'll explain later. Right now, Miracle, it's all about you."

Epilogue

The renovations on White Caps were done in the late spring, but the bed-and-breakfast didn't open for the season until the Fourth of July. Which was a conscious choice. The Moorehouse family was expanding so fast, it was all anyone could do to keep up with the changes. There were just so many moving vans and people coming and going....

Frankie and Nate decided to turn the whole barn into their private home. With the baby on the way, and more being hoped for, they knew they were going to need the extra space. Cassandra did all the planning work and Jay Dobbs-Whyte oversaw the on-site efforts. Frankie and Nate spent the first night in their new house at the end of June, a week before the B&B reopened for business.

Meanwhile, Joy and Gray bought a lovely duplex in Manhattan's famed Dakota Building. Joy's ball gowns were so popular with the New York City fashion set that she was besieged with commissions. Unable to handle all the work herself, she opened a small atelier in the garment district and hired two assistants, one who was good with shears and the other who was good with the phone. Gray accepted a teaching position at Columbia in the university's political science department and authored a book on electoral theory that was very well received. Every weekend, without fail, the two of them flew upstate in their jet and landed at the Glens Falls airport. The drive to Saranac Lake from there was just about two hours. If Gray was behind the wheel.

As for Alex and Cass, they bought a house on the lakeshore three mansions down from Gray's and four over from White Caps. The place was in absolute disrepair, a relic of the roaring twenties that had bats in its bedrooms and sagging floors and bathrooms that didn't work. It was, in Cass's words, absolutely beautiful. They stayed at Gray's during the renovations and planned to be there until their baby was born sometime at the end of September. By early winter they hoped their renovations would be finished, but again, Cass wasn't doing any on-site work. She was on bed rest, but tolerating the immobility well. As for Alex, he and the Norwich brothers began making sailboats. Now that Alex's cast was off, he was able to drive himself wherever he wanted to go. Which somehow was never far from Cassandra.

On May 10, Alex and Frankie and Joy paid their respects to their parents by going up the mountain behind White Caps and visiting Ted's and Mickey's graves. The three of them planned to do that yearly, now.

And on the first Saturday of every month, without fail, Nate and Spike spent the afternoon cooking up a huge feast. Alex picked up Grand-Em from Evergreen Assisted Living at five o'clock sharp, and the whole family sat down together to share the ins and outs of their lives. The talk was loud, the laughter frequent, the food delicious. And houseguests and friends were always welcome, so sometimes Sean showed up, too. As did Libby and Ernest.

After all, there was always a seat at the Moorehouse table for anyone who needed a place to put themselves. And the good was always better and the bad more bearable when you knew you were among friends.

Which was just as it should be.

* * * * *

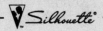

SPECIAL EDITION™

BABY BONDS

A new miniseries by
Karen Rose Smith coming this May

THE SERIES BEGINS WITH
CUSTODY FOR TWO

Shaye Bartholomew had always wanted a child,
and now she was guardian for her friend's
newborn. Then the infant's uncle showed up,
declaring Timmy belonged with him.

Could one adorable baby forge a
family bond between them?

And don't miss
THE BABY TRAIL,
available in July.

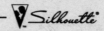

SPECIAL EDITION™

Luke Tucker knew he shouldn't get involved.

"Mary J. Forbes is an author who really knows how to tug on the heartstrings of her readers."
—*USA TODAY* bestselling author Susan Mallery

TWICE HER HUSBAND
by *Mary J. Forbes*

What he and Ginny Tucker Franklin had shared was over, had been for ten years. But when she returned to town, needing his help, years fell away. All the loneliness of the past decade vanished.

He wanted her as his wife again.

Available May 2006 wherever books are sold.

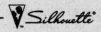

SPECIAL EDITION™

**Bound by fate, a shattered family renews
their ties—and finds a legacy of love.**

Family
BUSINESS

HER
BEST-KEPT
SECRET

by Brenda Harlen

Jenny Anderson had always known
she was adopted. But a fling-turned-serious
with Hanson Media Group attorney
Richard Warren brought her closer than ever
to the truth about her past. In his arms,
would she finally find the love she's
always dreamed of?

Available in May 2006
wherever Silhouette books are sold.

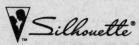

COMING NEXT MONTH

#1753 CUSTODY FOR TWO—Karen Rose Smith
Baby Bonds
It was a double blow to wildlife photographer Dylan Malloy—the sister
he'd raised died suddenly *and* didn't leave her newborn in his care.
Though her friend Shaye Bartholomew gave the child a good home,
Dylan wanted to help. He proposed marriage—but was it just
to share custody, or had Shaye too found a place in his heart?

#1754 A WEDDING IN WILLOW VALLEY—Joan Elliott Pickart
Willow Valley Women
It had been ten years since Laurel Windsong left behind Willow Valley
and marriage plans with Sheriff Ben Skeeter to become a psychologist.
But when her career hit the skids, she came home. Caring for an ailing
Navajo Code Talker, she began to work through her personal demons—
and rediscovered an angel in the form of Sheriff Ben.

#1755 TWICE HER HUSBAND—Mary J. Forbes
When widow Ginny Franklin returned to Misty River to open a
day-care center, she didn't expect to run into her first husband,
Luke Tucker—literally. The car crash with her ex landed her in
the hospital, but Luke considerately offered to take care of her children.
Would renewed currents of love wash away the troubles
of their shared past?

#1756 HER BEST-KEPT SECRET—Brenda Harlen
Family Business
Journalist Jenny Anderson had a great job in Tokyo and a loving adopted
family, but she'd never overcome trust issues related to her birth mother.
For Jenny, it was a big step to get close to Hanson Media attorney
Richard Warren. But would their fledgling affair run afoul
of his boss Helen Hanson's best-kept secret...one to which Jenny
held the key?

#1757 DANCING IN THE MOONLIGHT—RaeAnne Thayne
The Cowboys of Cold Creek
Family physician Jake Dalton's life was thrown into tumult by the return
of childhood crush Magdalena Cruz, a U.S. Army Reserves nurse badly
injured in Afghanistan. Would Jake's offer to help Maggie on her family
ranch in exchange for her interpreter services at his clinic provide him
with a perfect pretext to work his healing magic
on her spirit?

#1758 WHAT SHOULD HAVE BEEN—Helen R. Myers
Widow Devan Anderson was struggling to raise a daughter and run a
business, when her first love, Delta Force's Mead Regan II, suffered a
grave injury that erased his memory. Seeing Devan brought everything
back to Mead, and soon they were staking a new claim on life together.
But if Mead's mother had a say, this would be a short-lived reunion.